RAILROADED!

After the Civil War, German immigrant Helmut Rapp and his wife come to Kansas, claiming land under the Homestead Act. They battle the cruel elements, the Indian threat and the dangerous environment. Furthermore, Helmut has dark secrets of his own to fight. With the new railroad thrusting towards his land, Helmut strives to preserve the life and obscurity he has worked so hard to achieve. But mob violence, murder and revenge boil up, ripping his world apart and forcing him into a deadly duel . . .

MARK BANNERMAN

RAILROADED!

Complete and Unabridged

LINFORD
Leicester

First published in Great Britain in 2001 by
Robert Hale Limited
London

First Linford Edition
published 2003
by arrangement with
Robert Hale Limited
London

The moral right of the author has been asserted

British Library CIP Data

Bannerman, Mark
    Railroaded!.—Large print ed.—
Linford western library
1. Western stories
2. Large type books
I. Title
823.9′14 [F]

ISBN 0–7089–9481–4

Published by
F. A. Thorpe (Publishing)
Anstey, Leicestershire

Set by Words & Graphics Ltd.
Anstey, Leicestershire
Printed and bound in Great Britain by
T. J. International Ltd., Padstow, Cornwall

This book is printed on acid-free paper

For my good friends
Eric Hammond and Ian Johns

R.

1

Helmut's blood bay horse had finally given out, lameness in the left foreleg meaning that the relentless pace could be maintained no longer. He should have slipped the muzzle of his pistol beneath the beast's ear, pulled the trigger, but he did not. He was loath to kill an animal that had served him so well. He removed the saddle and bridle, cast them aside, and left the horse there, in the high grasses of the Kansas Prairie. Maybe it would recover. Maybe he would return for it later. But he felt this was unlikely. With Marshal Thomas Keno stalking him, he knew that the obscurity he sought was more elusive than ever. A confrontation seemed imminent, and against this man, whose skill with a gun was proven, his chances were limited. None the less, he swung his canteen-strap over his shoulder,

1

gripped the Navy Colt revolver and cleaved his way through the high grass towards the foothills. Once he reached elevated ground, and provided daylight remained, he might be able to spot Keno and see how far behind he was.

Helmut Rapp was forty years old and cursed with a name that had always reminded him of a flatulent stomach. He squinted into the sun. It was still brazen but soon it would settle into a westward drift, bringing relief from its intensity. He was a square-built man, heavy-featured, bushy-browed, his face showing red above a dark beard; his head was shielded by a forage cap, brought long ago from Europe. The shirt was dark with sweat, and his denim pants had buckskin reinforcements at seat and knee, neatly stitched by his beloved wife Delphinia. His eyes, bloodshot and narrowed, reflected the torment that the past days had brought him.

Concentrating on each step, not looking back at the head-drooped blood bay, he pressed forward, hoping that he would have the strength to attain the foothills, the start of the Ozark Mountains. Once there, he hoped he could find refuge in the forested highlands and gain the time he needed to reassess his position.

Earlier that day, after he had doubled back on his tracks then swung eastward, he had stopped at a tavern, a former way station, situated within a fork in the trail. Its broken sign proclaimed. JOE BENTWELL FEEDS THE HUNGRY AND CHEERS THE GLOOMY. The place was dilapidated. Half of it had been blown down by the wind and repaired with poles and factory cloth. But the half-dozen clients inside appeared unconcerned by the prospect that the establishment might collapse. The owner, Joe Bentwell, stood with his bulging middle pressed against a plank bar encrusted with fly-spots. He wore a shirt that had faded green stripes and huge sweat stains expanding out from the armpits. He slid a glass and a bottle of beer towards

Helmut, at the same time running an enquiring eye over him.

'Say, stranger,' he said, 'you ain't Rapp, are you? Helmut Rapp?'

Helmut slapped his coins on the bar-top, the sound coming sharply in the sudden quiet of the place. He sensed that all present were waiting for an answer to Bentwell's question.

Helmut uncorked the bottle and tried to disguise his Teutonic accent. 'Why? Who wants to know?'

'Oh, no offence, mister. It's just that Thomas Keno the marshal from Harvest Springs came through. Said he was looking for a Helmut Rapp. Said something about a big reward for his capture.'

Helmut nodded, saying nothing more.

Bentwell shrugged his shoulders, averted his eyes and busied himself wiping glasses. From behind him, his pale-faced, painfully thin, wife watched her husband as if she disapproved of everything he said and did. Helmut drank his beer, finding it akin to warm bathwater, so different from the foaming tankards he had once supped in the *biergartens* of Munich. He refilled his canteens from a cask of water and left the tavern, conscious of the stares that followed him. He wondered if Keno would realize that he had doubled back on his tracks.

Any hopes he cherished were dashed at noon that day. Topping a small, slickrock mesa, he reined in and gazed back across the prairie. It took a minute for his eyes to adjust. Wind caused the grass to swirl and dance. Eventually he spotted the movement of the lone rider, maybe a mile distant. The man's pace was relentless but unhurried. Perhaps he sensed that Helmut was weakening.

Helmut took a drag from his canteen, recorked it, and heeled the blood-bay onward, anger causing him to jerk the reins more roughly than was his habit. *Damn Keno! Why can't he let me be?*

Neither the pace of the prey nor that of the dogged hunter changed throughout the afternoon as they crossed sprawling grassland. Overhead, the sun burned, fierce as a sizzling branding-iron. Once, Helmut, lulled by heat and weariness, was startled by a loud hiss. He tensed as a black-headed coachwhip snake reared at him, then turned tail and retreated in short spurts, vanishing into the grass. If he paused for rest, he feared that Keno might catch him up and leap out with similar suddenness.

★　★　★

Now it was hours later and he was afoot, the blood bay abandoned, and before him were the foothills of the Ozarks, bare as weathered bones in the coming dusk. Helmut had fallen, cutting his thumb on a rock.

He wondered if he might find a cave or crevice on the slopes, somewhere to hide until the night fully took hold.

As he struggled on, his mind agonized over the past. Delphinia's last kiss that had left the taste of tears on his mouth. She would be disillusioned, heartbroken, her pride shattered by revelations that the marriage she had treasured was nothing but a sham. His daughter, Rosa, his little rose, set adrift in a world that would exploit her naïveté. The railroad bludgeoning its way through Coldwater Valley, destroying all his hopes. And gloating above everything, Ingrid's face, triumphant in the knowledge that she had finally gained revenge. He could have continued, compounding his misery. Instead, he tried to focus his concentration on survival.

The ground began to rise. His feet slipping on rocks, he climbed, glancing around in vain for somewhere to hide. Ahead, topping the slope, a perpendicular wall of rock, streaked with desert varnish, loomed and he figured he would have to go round this if he proceeded. He climbed on, gripping the revolver in one hand, using the other as support. The going became more arduous, he exhaled in great gushes and stopped. He hunkered down, exhaustion in his bones, again scanning his backtrail. Dusk was spreading its purple gloom, though not sufficiently to conceal any movement below him.

At first, as he saw nothing untoward, relief lifted his spirits, but then the clatter of a pebble drew his attention and he groaned. He had been looking in the wrong place. His adversary was far closer than he had imagined, riding through the shadows at the base of the escarpment, momentarily disappearing behind a screen of cottonwood.

Helmut goaded himself into action. He at last located a shallow, arid draw, running across the face of the slope. He dropped into it, fearing that Keno would have little trouble finding him . . . unless darkness somehow provided salvation.

His fingers were trembling and blood oozed from his cut thumb; he checked the revolver. He had stolen it from Keno. It had a chequered ivory grip and two .38 bullets in the chamber. He stifled his breathing, listening, not daring to lift his gaze above the rim of the draw. He felt like a trapped beast.

He had no real wish to kill Keno, or anybody else, but he knew that it would be a case of kill or be killed. He also knew that his own efforts would be clumsy compared with the ruthless ease with which the lawman handled his gun.

He shivered. The thickening night was almost tangible, seeping about him with a coldness that turned his sweat to ice. Time passed. He could hear the watch ticking in his pocket. It seemed loud but he knew it was his nerves making it sound so. Darkness prevented him from checking the hour, but he was conscious that each tick signalled he had one second less to live.

His vision was restricted to the sky and he watched the stars bloom against their velvety backdrop and wondered what lay beyond. He considered praying, but it seemed Janus-faced because he had quit the Lutheran church twenty years ago, convinced that it was not he who had deserted God, but God who had deserted him. The only prayers he had since offered had been for his daughter Rosa as she grew towards womanhood with a brain that was not right.

He wished he had shared Delphinia's faith and knelt alongside her when she had begged forgiveness for her sins, minor as they were. But then he recalled how, in the end, her prayers had achieved little because the family had been overwhelmed by something she had never suspected. *His* sins.

Presently his eyelids drooped.

The voice boomed through the night. It jarred him awake, sounding like a wrathful God. '*Helmut Rapp, come out. I know where you are!*'

His heart was beating so fiercely, he felt it would burst his ribcage.

2

It was twenty years earlier. Munich,
Bavaria, basked in an unseasonably
warm spring, and families strolled
along the streets, formally dressed and
enjoying the scent of the cherry-
blossom trees. The young Helmut
Rapp, of Bavarian-Swabian descent,
toiled over long columns of figures as a
bank clerk, perched on a high stool and
uncomfortable in his stiff white collar.
Sometimes he dreamed of a different
way of life, of wide spaces and fresh air,
and his widowed mother had told him,
'You should have been a farmer,
Helmut.' But Munich did not offer
such employment, and he would never
leave his mother with whom he shared
the house on Leipziger Strasse. He was
still trapped in the extremes of youth,
his spirits far from subdued by the
atmosphere at the bank. He enjoyed

spending the evenings with his friends in the *biergarten*, sometimes listening to intellectual and political conversations, and sometimes getting drunk, much to his mother's disapproval.

One evening he noticed Ingrid Obermeier for the first time. She was a singer at the Kelheim *bierkeller*. She flirted with the menfolk, head back as she laughed, tossing her blonde braids, swirling her skirts, casting her blue eyes far and wide. Helmut had never seen such blue eyes. He was so smitten with her that he became a regular visitor at her *bierkeller*, always occupying the same position, applauding madly every time she sang. At night, he dreamed of unlacing her bodice and drowning in the fullness of her pale breasts. He himself was a handsome, well-dressed young man of stocky build, and his adulation could not go unnoticed. Soon, as she finished each song, Ingrid would join him, resting her head upon his shoulder, pressing herself so close that he could smell her. By the summer, she was accompanying him to the opera, to art galleries, museums, and on boat trips along the Isar. He felt proud, walking arm in arm with her, attracting envious glances.

And one evening he unlaced her bodice, fulfilling his dreams in glorious ecstasy.

But his mother, a devout member of the Lutheran Church, did not approve of Ingrid. She warned Helmut that she would use him unmercifully and bring him only grief.

However, Frau Rapp was unable to influence her son for long. She suffered a tumour in the stomach and, three months after diagnosis, died at the *spital*. The last words she spoke were, 'Do not trust her, Helmut. She is a *hure*. She has no morals or gratitude. Do not throw your life away on that woman.'

Helmut had loved his mother and carried his bereavement for many years, but he could not tear himself away from Ingrid. He knew she teased other men, and he was jealous. He proposed to her in the belief that marriage would curb her excesses. To his delight she agreed to become his wife — on the condition that he raised no objection to her continuing as a singer at the *bierkeller*. Reluctantly, he acquiesced, feeling that it was a necessary exchange for capturing the hand of such a vivacious woman. They were married in a Roman Catholic church, as she wished.

At first things went well. They occupied the house on Leipziger Strasse, now owned by Helmut. He continued to work long hours at the bank, gaining promotion. She spent the days at home, rising late, not choosing to attend to domestic chores, preparing herself for evenings at the *bierkeller*. She spent money, buying dresses, hats, jewellery, knowing that he had inherited considerable wealth from his mother. She insisted on a servant, and to Helmut's surprise engaged a young man, scarcely more than a boy, rather than the maid he had anticipated.

Helmut soon became increasingly aware of her immense sexual appetite and matched her, learning aspects of passion he had never dreamed of. For a year he revelled in his private debauchery. But he was blinded to what was occurring when he was away, until one day he arrived home from work early, feeling unwell. Hearing laughter, he climbed the stairs and he caught Ingrid bedded with a man he had never seen before. The stranger leapt from beneath the sheet, grabbed his clothes and, clutching them about his nether regions, fled. Ingrid, now exposed, was naked apart from her frilly, silk garter.

Helmut was stunned, then he started to shout.

A row ensued. Ingrid flung his mother's precious ornaments at him, smashing them against the wall. She berated him for the stupid way he had trusted her. 'It was so easy to trick you, Helmut. No, he was not the only one. There were many, many others. You are so naïve.'

He stormed off to bed, rejecting his own bedroom where Ingrid had entertained her guest, going to the one that had belonged to his mother. He lay fuming and heartbroken, his pride shattered. But during the night, he heard his door open and she crept in and slipped into the bed beside him, pressing her warm body against his.

'I am sorry, Helmut,' she whispered. 'You'll always be my favourite man.'

He waited a long moment, cursing himself for being unable to resist her.

At last he said, 'Ingrid, promise me it will never happen again.'

'Of course, my darling.'

He was not sure whether 'of course' meant that it would never happen again, or it would, but as she caressed him he submitted to the passion that she was so expert in arousing. After all, she'd had plenty of practice.

Next day he knelt in the Lutheran church, his eyes moist with tears. He prayed, even pleaded, with the Almighty that Ingrid would mend her ways.

Sadly, any promises she made were of little value, though she gripped on to him like a leech, vowing she wanted no other man as her husband. Through the following weeks, he changed from a trusting spouse to a suspicious one, and he uncovered countless evidences of her daytime visitors. Soon, she had reverted to her old arrogant self, spurning him, and gradually he felt his faith in God waning.

The final straw came when, during the *Oktoberfest*, he caught her in bed, not with one man, but with three. All were naked.

'Come and join us, Helmut!' Ingrid cried.

'*Ja, ja!*,' one of her lovers shouted. 'It is so good!'

If Helmut had had a gun at that moment, he would have shot his wife, but instead he left the room, nigh slamming the door from its hinges. He tossed a few clothes and possessions into a valise and stormed from the house. That night he lodged at a local *gasthaus*. Next morning he drew all the money he had from the bank, handed his resignation to the astounded manager and told him that he had seen notices in the newspapers. The American government was seeking immigrants to populate the land. He was leaving Bavaria for ever.

★ ★ ★

Helmut booked a passage in Hamburg, having spent a hectic week arranging his emigration. All the while he feared that Ingrid might appear, screaming, ranting, making a scene, but she did not. He hoped that his former employer would not tell her of his intentions, not at least until he was half-way across the Atlantic.

The steamship proved to be a heavy, hulking brute that offered scant luxury. He had never been to sea before, and he encountered new smells and sounds. The thought of being cut off from land, at the mercy of the elements, brought the taste of fear into his mouth. But he suspected that many of the other passengers felt the same and he could not turn back now.

He shared a cabin with a sombre man who spoke continually of his skills as an undertaker and of the opportunities he would find in the New World. Helmut was glad enough to close his ears, occasionally giving a nod to imply his understanding. He spent much of the tedious crossing studying the German/English dictionary, memorizing numerous words. For long periods, he thus diverted his attention from the undertaker, the sea, his churning stomach and the fact that he could not swim. At night, visions of Ingrid's arrogant face taunted him, causing him to shout, waking both himself and his displeased companion.

Even though the sea was generally kind to them, he was glad enough when they at last sailed past Long Island into New York harbour, and the voyage was done, the ship finding her station at

Elephant Wharf.

It was December 1868, and relentless rain soaked the immigrants as they descended the gangplank. Helmut stood in line with the rest, frozen in his damp clothes, while forms were completed. Afterwards, they were checked for cholera and typhus, holding out their tongues for inspection by a doctor, and then released, laden with baggage, to establish their new lives.

3

'He's so handsome,' Delphinia Kelly said. 'Just looking at him makes my knees quiver!' Her voice was a warm Irish.

Delphinia was helping Olive Brackley turn a feather bed. She was employed by the Brackleys as a maid at their guesthouse in the small country suburb of Harlem in New York. Delphinia worked hard, and her employers were delighted with her, though her nature was outgoing and not remotely servile.

'But I understand he can't speak English,' Mrs Brackley remarked, pulling up the counterpane.

'That's not true,' Delphinia retorted. 'He has learned many words from the dictionary and he wants me to help him learn more.'

'And do you mind?'

'No, not at all. He has shown me

maps and papers. He is buying land in the West. He is going to be a farmer. He worked at a bank before, so it will be quite a change for him.'

'Rather him than me,' Olive Brackley said.

Delphinia Kelly was twenty-two years old, a slightly plump girl. Her face was round, portraying a regularity of feature, which, combined with her youthfulness, copper hair and a flash of green in her eyes, gave her an aura of prettiness. Life had not always been kind to her. Tragedy had struck when she was only eight. Her parents had been drowned in a boating accident, and being freshly emigrated from the Emerald Isle, there were no relatives to care for her. She had been sent to an orphanage in Albany where she had spent her growing-up years, firstly as a child and latterly as a carer for the other children. But circumstances had forced the orphanage to close, and Delphinia had come to New York and taken up employment at the Brackleys' guesthouse. She worked long hours, doing a great variety of tasks with cheerful Irish spirit, but she was generally free in the evenings. Having discovered that Helmut Rapp was anxious to learn English, she had offered to help him. Mrs Brackley had granted her permission to sit with him in the sitting-room of the guesthouse and she had set about the task, soon concluding that his company was immensely pleasant. At first she found him serious, awed by the strangeness of this new and immense country, but gradually her infectious cheerfulness crumbled his reserve and she had the feeling that he liked her. In return, she knew she had developed a real crush on him and had difficulty diverting her eyes away.

'Delphinia,' he once said, 'sometimes you look at me as if you could eat me.'

Her round face reddened slightly. 'I could,' she admitted and touched his hand. And they laughed together.

Her warmth, humour and outgoing

personality seemed to him like a lamp lighting up a shadowy world. The following week he kissed her for the first time. He was finding it easier to push memories of Ingrid and her scandalous behaviour to the back of his mind.

Once, quite tentatively, she had asked, 'Are you married, Helmut?'

He pretended not to hear, feigning a deep study of the English words she had listed for him — and she did not repeat the question then, apprehensive of the answer.

That night, when he lay in his bed away from Delphinia's happy spell, he cautioned himself. He must not hurt this rare, sweet girl, nor indeed entangle himself in more trouble.

He spent much time at the immigration-aid office. On its walls were countless posters proclaiming 'unlimited land opportunities'. In order to fulfil its ideal of 'manifest destiny', the US government had introduced the Homestead Act, whereby tracts of land were sold for settlement at incredibly low prices. In return, homesteaders, who could be of any nationality, were required to erect an abode in excess of twelve by fourteen feet, and live there for at least five years, farming the land. Helmut paid a paltry ten dollars for a section of land known as Coldwater Valley. It lay near the fledgling town of Harvest Springs in Kansas. He was granted well in excess of the normal one hundred and sixty acres plus free seed, due to the problems of farming on sloping ground. He knew that he might well regret taking such a chance on land that he only knew as a place on the map, but he was assured that he had got a bargain. 'The soil's so fertile out there,' the clerk explained, 'they say leaves and fruit grow on fence posts!'

At that price Helmut had little to lose, or so he thought.

He tried to cool his relationship with Delphinia, retreating into his old reserve, and he saw the resentment, the disappointment, rise in her. He rewarded her for her efforts in teaching him English with small meaningless, gifts — patterned handkerchiefs, confectioneries, scents. For several days, he bridled his inner feelings, telling himself over and over that their relationship, if allowed to grow, could only end with sorrow. And yet her presence reminded him of how shallow his love for Ingrid had been. He had been sucked into marriage by his vanity and by his lust. Now he had no affectionate feelings towards her. All that remained were an inner rebellion against the chains of matrimony and a resentment that he carried like a wound in his soul.

And then one Sunday, as they trudged through the snow along Fifth Avenue, admiring the fine brownstone houses, Delphinia posed again the question that was haunting her.

'Are you married, Helmut?'

He stopped, turned to face her, their breath freezing a cloud about them. Her hand grasped his firmly. She would not rest until she had the answer.

'Are you married?' she repeated.

He looked into her eyes, seeing the tautness of her emotion, knowing that he loved her above all else in the world and suddenly aware that he would rather die than lose her.

'No,' he said. 'I am not married.'

Happiness glowed from her. 'Then I will be your wife, Helmut, if you want me. I will come with you wherever you go.'

And she was suddenly in his arms, her kiss emphasizing her trust, numbing his conscience against the shame of his deceit.

Three weeks later they stood together at the Protestant church in Adams Street, and undertook the marriage ceremony. Mr and Mrs Brackley and two passers-by formed the entire congregation.

The rector's solemn words buzzed around Helmut's ears. 'I charge you both, as you will answer at the dreadful day of judgement, that if either of you know of any impediment why you may not be lawfully joined in matrimony you must now confess it. For be well assured that those as are coupled together, otherwise than God's word doth allow, are not joined together by God; neither is their matrimony lawful.'

Helmut could feel a pulse throbbing in his neck. His knowledge of English was still incomplete, but he gathered the meaning of the words clearly enough. He swallowed hard, maintained his silence.

Afterwards, the Brackleys signed the register as witnesses.

The marriage was consummated on the first night. Later, she lay in his arms like a carefree puppy.

'I am so proud to be your wife, Helmut. I feel safe now. It's like coming home after being lost.' Presently she told him that he was the first and only sweetheart she had ever known.

Half in English, half in German, he whispered his love for her, his commitment, and she drifted into contented sleep. It was a good hour before he knew the same peace. Europe, Ingrid and the past hovered in his mind. But they were a long way off. He must do everything to ensure that they remained so.

Five days later Helmut and Delphinia bade farewell to the Brackleys and boarded a train on the first stage of their adventure, the title-deeds to far-off Coldwater Valley in his pocket. They were totally unprepared for the awesome challenges that the next years would bring.

4

A land speculator called Sam Newcombe owned Harvest Springs. He had
been the first to see its potential when it
was nothing more than a cattle trail
through the buffalo grass, cleaving a
way towards the river-crossing. Within
three months of buying the land, he had
erected a row of tents. Soon came
unpainted, false-fronted buildings, and
beyond these, reaching out across the
prairie, appeared lines of building lots,
indicated by white stakes. Sam Newcombe believed that the cattle drovers
would come this way if his town could
provide ample facilities. It would be the
ideal river-crossing for herds coming up
from Texas and going north. They
would bring commercial profit. Soon,
the fledgling town would consolidate.
He dreamed of its houses, bank,
church, hotel, courthouse, telegraph

office, saloon and even a bawdy house. The last of these was of paramount importance if he was to attract the drovers. All would take root over the years. And so would settlement of the surrounding country. Each batch of starry-eyed homesteaders brought promise of prosperity for the town's tradesmen. But at present, Newcombe's plans remained in an embryonic state.

The Rapps had come by wagon westward from Kansas City and now they climbed stiffly down into Harvest Springs' only street, their feet sinking ankle-deep in dust, their baggage dumped beside them. The crudity of Western townships was nothing new, for they had encountered many over the past three weeks. The street was lined on each side by hitching rails, at which horses stood slip-shot, their tails flicking away the flies. The buildings boasted a multitude of signs, all different shapes and sizes, all proclaiming the business they offered, and women in poke bonnets walked the boardwalks with their children or stood talking to the storekeepers. There was something about this town, a sense of dynamism despite its humbleness, that quickened Helmut's interest.

Their journey had been long and uncomfortable, but not once had Delphinia complained. She was forever the ebullient, loving girl he had married, never stinting in showing happiness at her matrimonial state. They had travelled, by rail and stage, and both terrain and climate had changed about them. New York's bleakness gave way to spring's warmth, as they passed through Ohio and Illinois. Still further west, they crossed vast prairies, covered with bluestem, a seemingly endless succession of rolls, across which a freshening breeze blew. They encountered herds of buffalo, stretching as far as the eye could see. Later, they traversed land that was hilly and timbered with many creeks and springs, breathtaking in its beauty. And at night, no matter what their surrounds, he made love to her with a tenderness that he had never felt for Ingrid.

Now, they booked into the town's only hotel, The Westerners, which was little more than a log cabin with canvas extension, and next day, Helmut ensured that his stake was properly registered at the land office. After making inquiries, he engaged a carpenter and purchased timber to build his house. He then made arrangements to have workmen and raw materials hauled out to Coldwater Valley, fifteen miles away. Meanwhile, Delphinia bought groceries and hardware to start them off in their new home, showing an astuteness that made him proud.

Forty-eight hours later they left town, perched atop their timber on a wagon pulled by twin horses. The trail was narrow and so rough that at times they were nearly thrown off, but the horses plodded on, as unconcerned by the Rapps' precarious position as they were by the wagoner's whip. They passed through hills vivid with greenery and sunflowers, columbine and lupin, and ahead, roebucks pranced away, the sunlight catching the white flash of their rumps.

Helmut felt the blood pounding in his veins, for soon he would discover what he had committed them to.

Topping a last rise, they saw the valley for the first time and both Helmut and Delphinia gasped at the vision below them. For a moment, the wagon was stilled and they sat there, listening to the voice of silence, soaking in the view.

Coldwater Valley possessed a wide floor, thick with buffalo grass through which the river flowed. The water glinted invitingly in the sun and was bordered by cottonwood, black walnut, hickory, oak and gently rising sides.

Soon Helmut discovered the richness of the soil, it being soft to the toe. He had visions of cattle grazing, of the valley slopes rich with wheat.

'Oh, Helmut, my love,' Delphinia

gasped, her voice suddenly husky, her eyes shining. 'Our home . . . our home,' and he grasped her hand in his and their excitement was communicated like an electric current.

After the wagon creaked down the slope to the valley floor, Helmut and the carpenter spent a half-hour discussing where the cabin should be erected, eventually settling on a flat spot about one hundred yards up the slope from the east side of the river. It was here that the timber was unloaded from the wagon and their goods and chattels dumped.

'There's another family up the valley,' the wagoner told them. 'They won't trouble you none.'

Soon the empty wagon left them. Over the next few days it would return several times, bringing further supplies, tools, items of furniture. The carpenter, Jules Faury, a Frenchman, was of great assistance, helping and advising Helmut with his plans, cutting the timber, fashioning doors and window frames, ensuring that the measurements of the new house were unquestionably beyond the statutory 'twelve by fourteen'. And that afternoon, two further men arrived to help with the erection.

For the first two nights, Helmut and Delphinia slept in a tent. Thereafter, they had a timber roof over their heads. They had a stove with a chimney and gradually their new home took shape. Their neighbours, the Smithsons, a gaunt couple with a brood of children, came visiting. They did not say much nor stay long, merely emphasizing how hard the winters were, how harshly the government had treated them, and how the Osage Indians might go on the warpath any day and scalp them all. Helmut was quite relieved when they departed. He sought hope not discouragement.

The cabin had two storeys with a single room downstairs, and another upstairs which was divided by curtains and items of furniture. It was a solid structure with a timber frame and sloping roof. In addition, a barn, a two-hole privy, hog-pen and chicken-pen were built. Windows were covered with greased paper until glass panes could be afforded.

Over the next weeks, Helmut invested in twenty head of Hereford cattle, half a dozen hogs, some chickens, a goat for milking, and three horses, two to ride and one to pull a plough that he purchased. He bought glass for the windows to replace the greased paper. Meanwhile, Delphinia was never still, gathering cow-chips for fuel, cooking, sewing curtains, making cushions, organizing her pots and pans, picking wild flowers to decorate the main room, her 'woman's touch' making the cabin into a real home. Her face was radiant and she told Helmut that she had never been happier.

Spring stretched into summer and the heat settled into the valley. Helmut employed a man, Jack Bentley, to help him with the farming, tillage of the soil and planting of the seed that the government had issued. Bentley always seemed an old man, even when he was young. He was grey-haired, grey-moustached, squat and bow-legged, and a wizened brown. He slept in the barn and proved to be a good friend as time went by.

One day Delphinia said, 'Why is it the cows only graze for a little while, then they lie down? Are they sick?'

Old Jack Bentley smiled. 'They ain't sick, ma'am. There's so much goodness in the grass that they soon get satisfied.'

Helmut had now spent most of his money, and he knew that he could obtain nothing more from Bavaria. Future income would have to come from the land itself. Ingrid would have taken possession of the house in Leipziger Strasse, no doubt entertaining her countless guests. The thought made him flinch, and he wondered if his mother and father were turning in their graves. Delphinia told him that he sometimes talked in his sleep, and he vainly attempted to steer himself away from dreams of the past in case he revealed something that had to be kept secret. The prospect of shattering Delphinia's happiness horrified him.

But they were soon to learn that all their hard work, all their endeavours, were to receive a terrible set-back. It happened in the late summer.

One morning, when Delphinia was working at a tub of laundry in the yard, her arms and elbows deep in suds, she looked up to see strange silver spots in the sky. She brushed a strand of hair away from her eyes to make sure her senses were not playing tricks. She called to Helmut and he came running from the barn and soon they realized what the strange sight was — millions of grasshoppers in flight. In dismay they listened as the air throbbed with a roaring sound, increasing to almost deafening proportions. The light faded about them as the sky darkened. They ran back into the cabin, slamming the door and windows and from inside they watched the insects swarm down upon the land and heard them beating like hail against the cabin roof, walls, windows and door.

For an awesome four days, the grasshoppers ravaged everything they touched, eating, eating, eating. Even clothes hanging on a line were consumed. Trying to save the crops was futile and plants were denuded to their stalks. When Helmut spread blankets over his vegetable patch, the grasshoppers ate through them. The insects found their way into the barn and ate harnesses and hoe-handles. Helmut tied strings around his trouser legs to prevent the creatures from crawling up. They even invaded the cabin, settling on the table and chairs, clinging to the curtains and beds. At every step, they were crunched beneath the foot. Breathing became difficult because they were sucked in. They were everywhere, turning the world into nightmare. And then on the fifth day, the wind changed, and gradually the air thinned of the creatures.

Delphinia breathed a sigh of relief.

'My prayers have been answered!' she proclaimed.

But Helmut grimly concluded that those prayers had not saved them from the terrible devastation that the plague left behind.

Heartbroken, they walked the land, seeing how the crops had been ruined, how several of their cows had died, probably from suffocation in the smothering swarm.

A few days later they heard that the Smithsons had departed and gone back East, claiming they had been 'ruinated' by what had happened. But Helmut refused to be daunted. He had not come all this way to be defeated by grasshoppers. Scraping together the last of his money, he bought the land that the Smithsons had vacated. The entire valley was now his — for better or for worse.

Over three years of virtual privation, with the help of Jack Bentley, Helmut gradually restored his fortunes. Whenever his spirits sank, Delphinia was at hand to cheer him up, to make all the back-aching toil seem worthwhile. He never ceased to marvel at her fortitude and courage, and the fact that no matter how hard life was, her love for him, her pride in her marriage, grew stronger and stronger, and he wondered what he had done to deserve such a wonderful woman.

The harsh life toughened them both. They grew robust, drawing their strength from the land and adapting to the Western way, though Helmut retained the legacies of his Bavarian upbringing. But he now considered himself American, rather than European, and only rarely lapsed into his native German tongue. His English was improving, and he no longer had problems with his 'w's and 'th's. He even thought in English. His husbandry skills proved where his natural vocation had always been, and he sometimes wondered if he would still be sitting on a stool at the Munich bank if Ingrid had not turned his life around. Maybe he had at least one thing to be grateful to her for.

As for Delphinia: she appeared to revel in their Spartan life, finding all she needed in Helmut's love, her marriage — and her faith in the good Lord. She tried hard to restore her husband's religious convictions, but she sensed that there was some blockage in his past, which he was reluctant to explain. She did not probe, concluding that he would tell her everything when and if he was ready.

The day after her twenty-fourth birthday she was digging roots to make soap when she was startled by a loud whirring sound and simultaneously something stabbed into her wrist. Horrified, she gazed down to see the grey-tan scaly snake throwing back its head as if to strike again. She crouched, petrified, the rattling sound deafening. She held her breath, fearing that the slightest movement would cause the snake to dart towards her, but slowly it relented and slithered back, blending with the grass stems. Only then did she cry out for Helmut.

He came running, and she held up her wrist, displaying the two fang punctures. He slid his belt off and wound it around her forearm, just below the elbow. He drew it so tight that it bit into her flesh, bringing tears of pain to her eyes, but he told her to keep still. She waited while he ran back to the cabin and returned with a small, sharp knife. She did not flinch as he made a cut between the two punctures and then pressed his mouth to her wrist, sucking the venom, spitting it out.

When he was done, he wiped his arm across his lips. They both gazed at her wrist. It was swollen. He gathered her up into his arms and carried her back to the bed in the cabin. Her head was swimming, but the only pain she felt was from the tourniquet. She felt immensely tired and thought it was the poison in her body. He heated a linen rag in boiling water, waited a moment for it to cool and placed it on her wound. She cried out as it burned her, but he said, 'Be quiet or you'll drive the poison through your veins,' and she suffered in silence.

Within three days she was her normal self again, thankfully recovered. She thanked both Helmut and the Lord for giving her a good husband.

★　★　★

They became conscious of how Harvest Springs was developing. The false-front buildings had given way to permanent structures, there was now a bank and a saloon and countless stores, and most of the plots had been bought by people coming from the East. With satisfaction, Sam Newcombe could gaze over the town he had created.

Winters, sometimes severe, came and went, bringing snow and blizzards. It was in the second year that Delphinia announced she was pregnant, and they were so overjoyed that they waltzed around the cabin and sang at the top of their voices. Helmut made a cot on a rocker, and Delphinia knitted baby-clothes and blankets. And later, as her body swelled, she drew his work-roughened hand to the round curve of her belly so that he could feel the stirrings of new life.

Her time came and her waters broke. Helmut heeled his horse at speed to summon the midwife from Harvest Springs, but she was already involved with a birth and promised to come just as soon as she could. He then returned, hoping that the midwife would follow shortly. When she eventually reached the homestead three hours later, there was only the tidying up to attend to, Helmut having done his hamfisted best as the baby was born, even cutting the umbilical cord with the kitchen knife. Delphinia had been delivered of a daughter — and they named her Rosa Anna. Helmut cradled the babe in his arms, singing German nursery rhymes to her softly, calling her *Mein Kleines Röschen*, My Little Rose. For a while they revelled in the joy their baby girl brought them.

But Helmut was living on borrowed time. His past was stalking him, allowing him a brief period of respite before shattering his fool's paradise.

5

The motivation that brought Ingrid Rapp to the United States was something that had festered inside her ever since Helmut's departure. No man had ever turned his back on her in that way before, least of all a husband. Just as Helmut's pride had taken a sharp knock, so had hers. She learned from Helmut's former bank-manager, and subsequently the emigration office, that her husband had crossed the Atlantic. For some years she continued with her riotous existence, turning the house on Leipziger Strasse into a veritable brothel, even taking into employ a number of young girls for added attraction. But gradually her life began to cloy and she longed for wider horizons. Helmut returned to her mind over and over, and what she saw as the injustice he had done rose within her like a black wave.

She read everything she could about America, about the opportunities it offered. But these interested her less than the prospect of bringing Helmut to task for deserting her, and the challenge of it all grew in her until her mind was made up. In the spring of 1873, she sold all she had and followed in Helmut's footsteps, taking with her three pretty Bavarian girls who were willing to risk their chances in a far-off land. She learned some English words and persuaded her girls to do the same, particularly the words associated with love.

Once in New York, she made enquiries at the immigration aid office and from the records traced that her husband had bought land near Harvest Springs, Kansas. At this stage, it never occurred to her that he might have taken another wife. After all, what woman could compete with *her*!

On arrival in Harvest Springs, Ingrid discovered that Helmut Rapp owned land in Coldwater Valley, some fifteen miles distant. She also learned that he had a woman and baby. At first she felt aggrieved, but then she smiled to herself. This would enable her to make life even more difficult for him. She determined to play her cards carefully. Firstly, she needed to put down some roots of her own.

Ingrid and her companions noted that in town was the Buckthorn Saloon. It boasted that it was the best watering-hole west of the Mississippi and it appeared to be doing good business. It even claimed to have 'upstairs comforts', but she saw her chance here and sought out the saloon proprietor, a cigar-smoking man, Henry Claypole, a squatly built Southerner with a charming manner and a good eye for business. By the end of the day, he and Ingrid had hammered out a plan to expand the 'upstairs comforts' into an establishment worthy of Harvest Springs. Ingrid and her girls took up accommodation above the saloon and set about putting their ambitious plans into operation. Claypole was all too willing, bringing in builders to extend the building. Ingrid fuelled Claypole's dreams that, as the town increased in prosperity, he would create the most lavish whorehouse in the state of Kansas.

Strongly against such an establishment was Mrs Josephine Newcombe, the wife of the town owner. She had formed the local women's guild. Her husband Sam was a man of some moral conviction, but as a businessman, he knew that if the cattle drovers were to be attracted to the town, all tastes had to be catered for. He therefore gave Henry Claypole his full support.

★ ★ ★

A week later, Helmut was in town, collecting beans, flour, bacon, coffee and salt. He had left Delphinia and the baby at home. Rosa, nearly two years old, was giving them cause for concern.

51

She did not respond to them in the way children normally do and was not developing, showing neither inclination to crawl nor utter her first word-sounds.

Helmut had heard of the expansion at the saloon and a mild curiosity caused him to enter the place. It consisted of a huge room, with a great long bar lining one wall. Behind the bar was a mass of reflecting mirrors, which made the place seem double its size. He ordered a beer and carried the bottle to a table in an alcove. Men sat around playing poker, their eyes serious as they slapped cards down upon the green baize.

The Buckthorn Saloon had taken on a new lease of life since his last visit. Builders were busy extending the rear of the establishment, refurbishing the upper floor. Against a background of hammers and saws, he listened to the clink of glasses, the tinkle of the honky-tonk and the hum of voices about him. His interest quickened as he heard talk of the ambitious German woman and her girls who were intent on providing the establishment with high-quality creature comforts. His mind drifted to Ingrid. How she would revel in such a place! He tried to scoff at the idea. Surely it could not be . . . ? Even so, he felt uneasy.

Standing within a doorway on the balcony, she had seen him enter and watched him all along, her heart beating rapidly as she realized that her search was complete. She was filled with a triumphant sense. After all this time, he was within her grasp once again. The years had brought changes to him. He seemed bigger, having filled out considerably. He was heavily bearded, had been weathered by the elements and was even more handsome than she remembered. But it was unmistakably Helmut, still wearing his blue cap. *Her* Helmut! She turned, checked her blonde hair in a mirror, smiling as she concluded that a certain maturity had not decreased her attractiveness either. She went down the staircase.

Helmut had finished his beer, was stepping towards the door, when she called his name. At first he seemed not to hear, continuing his walk, but she called again and he stopped. When he turned, the colour drained from his face.

He tried to say, 'Ingrid!' but all that emerged from his mouth was a croak. Shock had dried his juices.

She was not tongue-tied. 'Helmut, my love, how wonderful to see you! I was so sad you left me. I was wicked. But now I will make it up to you, I promise. I will be a good wife from now on!'

All he could do was blink his eyes and then stare at her, hoping that the vision before him would prove some sort of mirage, a hideous dream from which he would awaken.

But nothing he could do changed the fact. Maybe she was a little thicker on the hips; maybe the blonde hair had lost some of its glint; but the eyes still possessed their deep blue, their same arrogance. This was the Ingrid he had hoped never to see again.

'Ingrid, how did you . . . ?' he at last managed.

'Are you not pleased to see me, Helmut? I have missed you so much.'

And she reached out, gripped his arm and pulled him against her, knocking his cap askew as she pressed her lips to his face, feeling the roughness of his beard.

When she stepped back for air, he drew a hand across his jaw and straightened his cap. He felt sick.

'We must talk,' he said.

'Of course. Let us find a table. We must celebrate.'

'*Nein!*' He was fighting to come to terms with his dismay. 'Not here. Somewhere private. There are things you must understand.'

She feigned a look of innocence, fluttering her eyelashes. '*Ja, ja*, there are plenty of things we must tell each other. I have a room upstairs. We will go there.' Helmut frowned. He had no wish to go to her room, but maybe it would be better than being seen with her in the saloon and word somehow getting back to Delphinia. He nodded, followed her through the crowded saloon and up the stairway, conscious of every inquisitive eye that was turned towards him, angry at the smug remarks, but not responding. His feelings were as bleak as those of a condemned man climbing the steps to the gallows.

She led him along a balcony over the saloon, then down a passageway to an end room. Inside were four unoccupied beds and several trunks, their lids thrown back to reveal assorted female clothing.

'Only temporary accommodation for me and the girls,' Ingrid said, 'until we get our proper rooms.' She turned, smiling. 'Now then, Helmut honey, it can be like old times.'

He was about to respond when a young woman burst in upon them, only to back out saying in German, 'Sorry, Ingrid.

Didn't realize you had company.'

Uneasiness increased in Helmut. The more people who knew that he had visited this woman, the more dangerous it would be. He could not stand the thought of Delphinia knowing about it. If she learned that her marriage was a sham, it could break her, even cause her to leave him. Ingrid could reveal him as a bigamist and bring the law down on him. And, furthermore, Rosa would be exposed as a bastard.

'Ingrid,' he said firmly, 'things can never be the same again. I have a wife now and — '

'A wife!' she retorted. 'I am your wife, Helmut. Always was, always will be. Only divorce can change that, and the Catholic Church does not permit that. Anyway, I'd never give you that satisfaction. No, you must send your fancy-woman packing.'

Helmut paced the room, breathing heavily, his jaw tight with anger. She had him dangling on the end of a line and she was enjoying it. Despite what she said, the only solution was divorce, he thought, or death! At last he turned to face her, seeing how the arrogant smile still widened her lips.

'I need time, Ingrid,' he said, 'time to think things through.'

She puckered her sensuous lips as she pondered, then she nodded. 'That's fair. I'll give you a week. You come back here in a week's time, eh? Tell me that you've got rid of your fancy-woman. Can't have you living in sin, Helmut. Bigamy's a serious offence, you know.' She laughed. 'Next time you come, we'll have the place a little more comfortable with more privacy. I'll show you what you've been missing all these years.'

He gave her a vague nod of agreement while his thoughts were racing, wondering how he could extract himself from this mess. One thing was certain: he must avoid hurting Delphinia, and he had just seven days to come up with a plan.

He turned away from her with a curt

nod. He found an exit at the rear of the building and left with only the workmen seeing him. He drove his wagon at an angry pace and was home before nightfall, Delphinia welcoming him with a warm kiss and supper on the table.

'What's wrong, honey?' she murmured, sensing that something was amiss.

He took her in his arms and whispered, 'Nothing,' in her ear.

6

For Helmut the next days passed in a whirl of uncertainty. On the third morning he rose and, still in his nightshirt, went outside to milk the cow. He cleaned the soft teats with a damp rag before squeezing long streams of warm, frothy fluid into an enamel bucket. He realized that Delphinia had stepped out from the cabin, was standing behind him.

'What's wrong, honey?' she asked him again. 'Your face has got the shadow of doom across it.'

Helmut was annoyed with himself for allowing his feelings to show. For a moment he wondered if he should tell her everything, but he could not stand the prospect of seeing her happiness crumble away. He felt he had no option but to continue with his deceit.

'I'm worried about Rosa,' he said.

'She just doesn't seem to be growing up properly.'

Delphinia gave him an odd look, her eyes showing a suspicion that there was more to his bleak mood than he was saying.

True enough, he was worried about Rosa, but it was the thought of Ingrid that was driving him to distraction. He sensed she was determined on making life for him as difficult as possible, and when he went to see her again he would have to come up with something to satisfy her. Otherwise, he knew she would make a scene, stir things up well and truly, and he and Delphinia would be done for. He tried to drive his worries away by working twice as hard at his chores, at the same time hoping that some plan would click into his mind, but he could think of nothing, apart from taking a gun with him on his next visit and doing away with the woman — but he was not prepared for that.

Delphinia was surprised when he

went into town so soon, for they were well stocked with supplies, but she never questioned him and kissed him goodbye with her usual warmth.

'I love you,' she whispered in his ear, and he gave her a hug, feeling sick and ashamed.

He left her and took the wagon into Harvest Springs. He believed that any revelation regarding his past would go completely against Delphinia's religious convictions. Her world would come crashing down, just as his would. He wished he had some solid plan in his mind, some way that would get Ingrid off his back, but all he could think of doing was to explain his circumstances to her. He would appeal for her compassion, but he had little hope that this would bring him joy.

A week had made quite a difference in the progress of the work at the Buckthorn Saloon. Painters had now taken over from the builders and carpenters and the whole place was looking spruce. He went up the back stairs and along the corridor to Ingrid's room. A rap on the door brought no immediate response, but one of the other girls approached along the corridor, saw him and said in German that she would fetch Ingrid.

'Who shall I say wants her?' she enquired.

'Helmut.'

She gave him a slight smile and he wondered if she shared the confidences of her mistress.

Within five minutes, Ingrid appeared and greeted him with a welcoming laugh. 'Expected you to come in the front way,' she said.

Soon they were seated inside, she on her bed and he on a chair, and she asked him what plan he had come up with. He told her that he had a very dear person as his second wife and that the last thing he wanted was to hurt her.

'I would like to meet this *marvellous* woman,' Ingrid said. 'Is she so much better than me? I bet she doesn't satisfy you like I used to. And like I *will* do, Helmut.'

He made no response. He knew he was boxed into a corner. Presently he said, 'If it's money you want, Ingrid, I'll pay.'

The old arrogance was upon her. Her laugh was dismissive. 'Oh, it's not just money, Helmut. It's more than that.' She had been toying with the buttons on the front of her dress, now she slipped them undone, revealing the swell of her pale bosom. 'You know you can't resist me,' she whispered. 'You never could.'

She grasped his hand, pressed it to her breast. He cursed himself for he could feel her warmth and his old passions stirred and her laugh came again, this time softly. He pulled his hand away.

'If we can reach an agreement,' she said, 'maybe we could meet once a month, just for old time's sake. You can make me a monthly allowance of, say, a hundred dollars.'

He felt his innards squirm at what she was suggesting. He knew very well what 'visiting' her meant. The thought of leading an adulterous life, of deceiving Delphinia, was hideous. Furthermore, he could ill afford to pay what she suggested.

'And if I refuse?' he demanded.

Her lips curved into a triumphant smile. 'I shall tell everybody that you are my husband.'

He sighed deeply. What he needed was time. If seeing Ingrid each month, paying her an allowance, was the price he had to pay, maybe he could live with it, until he came up with some other plan. And pray to God Delphinia would never know.

'A monthly visit,' she murmured, savouring the idea, 'say the last Monday of every month. And it need go no further than you and me. Don't look so sad, Helmut. A lot of men would welcome the idea.'

He gave his head a slow, reluctant nod, but she was not going to allow things to rest at that.

'And there's something else, Helmut. I have been thinking. You bought land cheap at Coldwater Valley, eh?'

'Ja,' he murmured, fearful of more demands from her.

'And I know the price of land is going up around here,' she said. 'As a final gesture of good will from you, Helmut, all I ask is that you consign the land over to me. Thereafter, I'll let you and your so-called wife live there in peace, until I need the land.'

'That could be tomorrow!' he gasped.

'No. I won't claim it until it is necessary. At present things are going well for me.'

He had taken a sharp intake of breath. 'I cannot do that, Ingrid. That land belongs to Delphinia and me. It's our security for the future.'

Again she laughed. 'Would you rather I spread word about how I am your real wife? How you have committed bigamy? As I said, I will let you live on the land for the foreseeable future.

Maybe I will change my name. Something more American than Rapp. Never was much of a name. If I had a different name, people wouldn't suspect you and me were . . . related. Just sign the land over to me, come and see me every month with the money and everything will be all right.'

He gazed at her. He did not trust her one iota, yet what option did he have?

She stepped close to him, slipped her hands on to his shoulders, meeting his eyes. 'Do as I say, Helmut.'

'How do I know,' he said, 'that if I agree your terms, you still won't tell all and sundry that you're my wife?'

'Helmut,' she answered reproachfully, 'you'll have my word.'

'Damn you, Ingrid,' he said, but she smiled at him.

Gazing into her face, he controlled an urge to sweep her over his knee and slap her pretty backside.

'Do as I say, Helmut,' she repeated softly.

He swallowed the bitter taste that

had come to his mouth. And then, at long last, he acceded to her wishes.

The following week she was with him when he had the solicitor in town make the deeds to Coldwater Valley over to Ingrid. Helmut insisted that the man swore not to breathe a word about the transaction to anybody.

⋆ ⋆ ⋆

Time slipped away. Helmut made a monthly journey to town to collect supplies and keep his appointment with Ingrid. To his chagrin, he found it not as unpleasant as he had anticipated. She had lost none of her skills. And as she ensnared him in her passionate web, she was able to keep her claws into him, to retain an intimacy that he could not deny, a constant reminder that she held the whip hand. Meanwhile, she turned her bawdy house at the Buckthorn Saloon into a high-class establishment, bringing in more girls from Bavaria, all of the prettiest appearance. She was in her element, had never been happier. Her partnership with the saloon-owner Henry Claypole was proving a good business deal, and their relationship went much further than business. A semicircular stage with footlights and plush red curtains had been erected at one end of the great bar-room and it was from this that Ingrid, who had now renamed herself 'Abigail Brown', blew extravagant kisses to her audience, and entertained with her songs, sometimes bawdy, sometimes mawkish. She was often backed by her dancing girls, all clad in the flimsiest of costumes.

A carpeted staircase led up from the saloon to the first floor, where a long balcony overlooked the great room on three sides. A sign was pinned to the wall, striving for propriety. It read: COWBOYS MUST REMOVE SPURS BEFORE BEING SERVICED. SATISFACTION GUARANTEED OR MONEY BACK.

Off the balcony was a large room. Two magnificent chandeliers, each with twenty or more candles, hung from the ornate ceiling. The walls glinted with mirrors, as well as being adorned with Renaissance paintings of wistful ladies, all in various stages of undress — but it was the real-life girls who drew the eye. The town had never known such concentrated femininity. The girls would sit round on richly brocaded sofas, their red-lipped smiles focused on their visitors, their dresses plunging low to reveal their pale European bosoms, their accents seductively Germanic. One was usually nursing a small, fluffy dog called Fritz. To men fresh from weeks of hardships on the range, they seemed like angels of joy come down from heaven.

Through a further doorway another corridor extended, all lushly carpeted. Numerous smaller rooms led off. It was here that the girls entertained their guests. Each room was dimly lit, and possessed a bed covered with cushions. There was also a chair, a small chest of drawers, and upon this stood a water jug and washbowl. On the floor was a thunder-mug decorated with floral patterns. All were best quality items imported from the East.

The local Women's Guild, headed up by Sam Newcombe's wife, was strident in condemning the establishment, but Newcombe himself only acknowledged their objections with an understanding nod and allowed matters to proceed. The town needed a good bawdy house, and he was determined to offer a top grade facility.

As the years slipped by, Helmut and Delphinia braved the hardships of working the land, the elements, prairie fires, and other setbacks with fortitude. For a whole week they barricaded themselves in while Osage Indians camped in the valley, slaughtering their cows and firing arrows into the cabin door. Helmut eventually drove them off with a fusillade of gunshots and they never returned.

He gave to his second wife all the love in his soul, hoping that it would in some way make up for the way he was deceiving her, but the situation often got to him and he had spells of depression. He guessed he would somehow scrape together the monthly payment that Ingrid demanded. Delphinia had always left the handling of financial affairs to him, and he doubted that she would ever wonder why they were not as well off as they ought to be.

Things were not helped by the other great concern of his life. By the time Rosa learned to walk and utter her first words, she was nearly three, and it was obvious that her brain was somehow damaged. Helmut would sometimes have a tear in his eye as he bounced his 'little rose' on his knee, or read her fairy stories, which she failed to comprehend. Remembering his frantic fumbling at her moment of birth, he wondered if the harm had been caused by the fact that his only previous experience of birthing had involved calves and piglets. He could not tell. All he knew was that the thought remained with him like a tumour.

He and Delphinia took Rosa to the doctor in town who explained to them that her brain was permanently damaged and she would never be like other children, but he tried to console Helmut by telling him that the problem had not been the result of a mishandled birth. Rosa would never be fit enough to attend normal school. So Delphinia herself tried to teach her numbers and reading, but it was all too complicated for the child. As she grew older, her body growth quickened, as if angry with itself for starting off slowly, and by the time she was twelve, she could have been mistaken for a full-grown woman, except for her simple mind. Delphinia dressed her in pretty clothes, and on the rare occasions Helmut took his family to town, Rosa attracted the eyes of many young men until they realized she was strange. Both parents were saddened by the prospect of what awaited their daughter, particularly when they were no longer around to look after her.

7

It was seven years after Ingrid's arrival at Harvest Springs. Certain members of the Women's Guild were almost fanatical in their condemnation of the town's outrageous whorehouse, and were ashamed by the way the girls flaunted their bodies, claiming it was degrading the female sex. They had no words ugly enough to express their scorn. Many wives would turn their eyes rather than look at 'that awful German woman' as she paraded down the street, twirling her parasol and arching her eyebrows. Sometimes she and her girls even had the nerve to attend church service.

The closeness between Ingrid Rapp and Henry Claypole, owner of the saloon, had increased and it was rumoured that he insisted that she reserved her favours for him alone, leaving the entertaining of other men to the German girls. So obsessed with Claypole had Ingrid become that she willingly complied and Helmut was able to escape his monthly visit. She even agreed to forgo her monthly allowance, having no need for the money now.

It was in the early hours of a Monday night in August, 1877, that the Buckthorn Saloon caught fire. Nobody ever knew who or what started it, though fingers were later pointed at the Women's Guild. They steadfastly denied any wrongdoing.

The blaze erupted from some old boxes at the rear of the premises, seizing on to the tinder-dry wood of the outside stairs and balcony. Within minutes flames, fanned by a south-west wind, were leaping into the night sky and the saloon girls were rushing about in their night-clothes, screaming, their faces smeared with soot and flying sparks. They clutched at the few possessions they were able to grab, including the poodle-dog Fritz that yapped incessantly. Henry Claypole bravely defied the heat to rescue Ingrid, who had been trapped in her room. Carrying her in his arms, he scrambled down the stairway amid leaping tongues of flame and bore her to safety. By the time the town stirred from its slumbers, the situation was out of control. The volunteer fire-brigade had proudly set up its efficient man-powered fire-pump, but then found it had insufficient hose to get anywhere near the flames and could do little more than watch the rear of the saloon cave in. People formed chains in the smoke, passing buckets of water; others struggled with shovels and wet gunny-sacks, but before any effect was felt, the establishment was a smouldering wreck. It was a miracle nobody had perished. While the men took delight in consoling their heartbroken, sooty-faced 'angels of joy', members of the Women's Guild stood at a safe distance, smiling smugly and calling the fire 'the wrath of God'.

At first it even seemed that 'the awful German woman' had received an extra punishment for her sins. Ingrid had inhaled smoke and for several days she completely lost her voice but, all too soon for some, it returned, although her singing never again had the 'trill' that had once been its charm. However, some men claimed her new husky tone was even more seductive than of old. And there was something else. Her obsession for Henry Claypole had pushed her old anguish against Helmut into the background.

Overall, the 'respectable' ladies of Harvest Springs had little cause for satisfaction. Within six months, Henry Claypole and Ingrid Rapp, or Abigail Brown as she was now known, had the establishment completely rebuilt, its style even more lavish and voyeuristic than before. Firecrackers were let off in celebration. The grand re-opening lasted a whole week and was an occasion of shameless revelry. Later, horse-racing was introduced down the main street, and heavy betting took place, but local killjoys had ditches dug across the thoroughfare and put a stop to it. Meanwhile, the fire brigade obtained lengthier hoses.

Sam Newcombe watched his town grow more prosperous, and knew that only one further facility was needed — the railroad.

And that was coming closer by the day.

* * *

A month after Rosa's fourteenth birthday, Helmut had stepped outside on to the porch, seeing how purple shadows of evening were spreading across his field of Turkey Red wheat, the grains for which he had purchased from some Mennonites. The gentle lowing of the milch-cow sounded from down in the meadow and the hogs and chickens had bedded down for the night. Rosa was in the chicken-coop. She liked to gentle those birds of an evening, even wept when one had its neck stretched.

Suddenly Mattie the collie dog started barking. Helmut glanced up the valley and saw why. Two riders were approaching. They reminded him of black crows. The dusky light somehow shrouded out the legs of their horses, so that they appeared to be floating on air. Helmut shuddered. He had expected a visit for some days, though he had tried to convince himself that it would not happen.

He realized that Delphinia had come to stand at his side and watch the approaching riders. 'Marshal Keno,' he said. 'I don't know who the other fellow is.'

Thomas Keno rode slightly ahead of his companion. He was town marshal of Harvest Springs and had a reputation as a hard man who had killed more than once. His long black coat sagged open to reveal a scarlet shirt and the two ivory-butted pistols belted at his hips in cross-draw fashion. He had a narrow face and a long nose with a kink half-way down. A waterfall moustache hid his lips, and his eyes had a habit of darting everywhere, as if seeking out trouble.

As they drew close, Helmut could see that the second rider also wore a long coat, but he was a short, fat-bellied man with bushy sideburns. He was wearing a derby hat and his shrewd porcine eyes peered at the world through oval-shaped spectacles.

Thomas Keno raised his arm in greeting. 'William Greygoose to see you, Helmut,' he said in his deep voice. 'He's the representative of the M. and P.C. Railroad, come to make you a proposition. While he's doing that, we could sure use a drop of coffee.'

Greygoose dismounted clumsily from his horse, his short legs having difficulty in locating the ground. Once afoot, he stepped forward, his plump face wreathed in a smile, his hand extended towards Helmut.

'It's an honour to meet you, Mr Rapp. I think you'll be very pleased with what I've got to offer.'

Helmut nodded curtly, shaking the railroad man's hand without warmth. He felt sick in the gut. The railroad officials had probably inspected the government records. These had never been changed to Ingrid's name. It was only the deeds held by the solicitor in Harvest Springs that showed the change. These men were clearly under the impression that Helmut still owned this land and, in front of Delphinia, he would have to play them along. A moment later, their horses were hitched at the watertrough and the visitors stood in the main room of the cabin while Delphinia poured the coffee.

'Nasty red mark you got on your face, ma'am.' Keno grinned. 'The ol' man been hitting you?'

'No,' she replied testily. 'An accident with the wash-boiler.'

The marshal's smile widened in disbelief. The man's arrogance made Helmut uncomfortable. His eyes were probing into every corner of the room.

After a slurp of coffee, Greygoose

said, 'Now perhaps we can talk business, Mr Rapp. You've probably heard how the railroad is running a line through this country. Harvest Springs will be the most important stopping point. The railroad'll open up this land and bring tremendous prosperity to everybody, including yourself, once I've made you the offer.'

'Offer?' Helmut queried, his lips a hard line within the tangle of his beard. Delphinia gazed at the railroad man, the inkling as to the purpose of this visit taking hold in her mind.

'Why yes,' Greygoose said. 'You'll appreciate that this valley is the obvious route for the line to run through. Otherwise we'd be building rails across mountains.' He somehow saw this as a joke and unleashed a laugh in which Helmut did not join.

'Yes, across the mountains,' Keno remarked, thumbing back his hat and raising an eyebrow. 'That would be real crazy.'

Greygoose continued. 'Yes, yes. So

the line will run through this valley. The company will pay good money for the land.' He looked at Helmut. 'You'll be most generously compensated, Mr Rapp.'

Helmut's response came with the finality of a nail being driven into the lid of a coffin. '*Nein*!'

'But you've not heard how much the company'll pay you,' Marshal Keno said. He drained his coffee-cup. 'You'll change your mind when you hear.'

Greygoose had extracted an official-looking paper from the inside pocket of his coat. 'All we need is your signature.' He flattened the document upon the table, adjusted his spectacles and read aloud. 'For the purchase of all rights on the land known as Coldwater Valley, the M. and P.C. Railroad will pay to the present owner the sum of twenty-five thousand dollars — '

'Twenty-five thousand dollars!' Delphinia's shocked gasp caused Greygoose to pause, a smile widening his lips.

'I knew you'd be impressed by the offer, Mrs Rapp.'

Delphinia was amazed at the generosity of the offer. With that sort of money, they could set up home in a new place and still have plenty left over.

Helmut felt as if an icy hand was gripping his heart. The pretence he had maintained over the last fourteen years was under threat of being blown apart. Indignation fuelled by fear made his face tingle.

'Impressed!' Helmut cried out. 'We're disgusted. Understand, Mr Greygoose, there was nothing in this valley when we first came — just wilderness. We cut timber and built this home with our own hands. We raised our child here, schooling her ourselves because the schoolhouse was too far away. We tamed the land, saved up and bought our stock. We came through a grasshopper plague, Indian trouble, drought, blizzards and sickness. And you can be sure of one thing. We are not moving — not for the railroad, not for anybody else. Not even for five hundred thousand dollars!'

Delphinia was looking at him with amazed eyes.

The smile had gone sour on the face of William Greygoose. His lips trembled with consternation.

Marshal Keno showed no such agitation. His deep voice came as an awesome warning, dropping the familiarity of Helmut's first name.

'You got to be reasonable, Rapp. The railroad means progress, and you can't stop progress. It'll bring prosperity to a lot of folks. They ain't gonna take kindly to you blocking the way.'

Delphinia and the wide-eyed Rosa had gathered behind Helmut, tightening together as a family unit. Conscious of Keno's stare, Delphinia fastened the top button of her daughter's nightdress.

Helmut's bearded jaw was thrust forward. '*Nein*!' he shouted. 'We will not sell the land. Now go. Leave us in peace.'

Greygoose gathered up his paper,

refolded it with angry hands, stuffed it into his pocket, and said, 'Matters won't be allowed to rest.'

Keno placed a hand on the butt of his revolver suggestively. 'The railroad won't take no for an answer, Rapp, you can be sure of that. The surveyors have plotted this valley already. They'll come back within a day or so to finish their plans.'

Greygoose started to say something but Helmut's hostile glare silenced him. The railroad man sighed heavily, turned his back and stomped from the cabin.

Keno leered at Delphinia, then his eyes drifted to Rosa, lingered for a long moment. 'Right pretty daughter you have,' he murmured. 'I sure hope nothing bad ever happens to that sweet body of hers.' He put a finger to his hat in mock courtesy and departed, Mattie the dog baring her teeth as he passed. For a second the only other sound was the thump of Keno's boots on the porch planking, the jingle of spur-rowels. This gave way to the creak of saddle-leather and the receding thud of hoofs in the soil.

Delphinia was the first to move, gathering up the empty cups. 'Helmut, that's marvellous money they're offering. I could hardly believe my ears. We should take it and move. There's still plenty of other land to be had. If we don't, they'll make trouble for us, for sure.'

Rosa's lips widened into a wistful smile. 'The marshal said I was right pretty,' she whispered.

Helmut walked across the room and lifted his .44 calibre Winchester rifle from its pegs on the wall. He checked the mechanism, ran his fingers across the octagonal barrel. 'Remember when we drove off the Indians?' he said. 'We'll see off the railroaders too!' He paused, letting his words sink in, his face taut, a vein in his forehead pulsing, then he added, '*Ja*, I'll fight them if I have to.'

He was conscious of Delphinia's shocked eyes staring at him, and the unspoken word on her lips . . . why . . . why?

After a moment she said, 'Helmut, I don't understand.'

Helmut crossed over to her, wishing he could explain everything, but knowing he could not. He placed the gun down upon the table and took her in his arms.

'Whatever happens,' he said, 'I won't let anybody harm you, my love.'

8

It was three evenings later. In the courtroom above the marshal's office, the mayor, John Dilly, was presiding over a meeting of the town council of Harvest Springs. Whiskey was flowing freely and the air was thickened by cigar smoke. Moths fluttered about the gas-lamps. Through the open window, a tinkling piano, raucous voices and laughter sounded from the down-street Buckthorn Saloon. As usual business was booming.

Gathered around a table, in addition to the mayor, were Sam Newcombe, Seth Mason the justice of the peace and editor of the *Harvest Springs Herald*, Floyd Cresswell who owned the local bank, Matt Warner who ran the Westerner's Hotel, and Thomas Keno, the marshal. All had been elected to public office. Sam Newcombe ran his town along democratic lines. In consequence, they showed him a marked deference. Also present was the plump William Greygoose representing the M. & P.C. Railroad.

Sam Newcombe managed the Harvest Springs Land Company. He was now approaching fifty. His hair showed a distinguished grey, and a shrewd expression did not diminish the handsomeness of his face. In addition to his good looks, he had the important advantage of owning the town. Harvest Springs had now consolidated, with its houses, bank, church, hotel, courthouse, telegraph office, saloon, bawdy-house, stores and even its own newspaper; all had taken root over the years. But Newcombe had greater dreams for the town. With its ample supply of water and space for cattle-pens, Harvest Springs could become the link between the Chisholm Trail and the railroad. This would change the nature of Harvest Springs, and bring immense prosperity to those who lived here.

'Gentlemen,' William Greygoose said, 'I have to report that all landowners in this territory have accepted the railroad's terms and will be vacating their homesteads.' He cleared his throat. 'That is, all except one. The German Helmut Rapp has refused to give up his land in Coldwater Valley. I found him to be a fierce and unreasonable man.'

Newcombe removed the Havana cigar from his mouth. 'Then why don't you offer him double? We'd finance the difference from town funds. I guess the wheels of progress need greasing sometimes.'

'Rapp wouldn't change his mind if you offered him a million,' Greygoose stated. 'He's the most stubborn man I've ever come across.' He paused, letting his words sink in, then he went on. 'You must realize that if we can't run the track through Coldwater Valley, we'll have to bypass Harvest Springs altogether. The president of the construction team has made it quite clear.'

'That,' Sam Newcombe said, 'is unthinkable. We all know that Harvest Springs is the nearest point in the entire state to the Chisholm Trail, and the cattle herds will come in force if there's a railroad. The project will be worth millions to this town.'

There was a murmur of excitement around the table.

'One thing's certain,' Floyd Cresswell the banker said. 'We can't let Rapp stand in our way.'

'Then how can we move him?' Mayor Dilly's question hung in the air. Glances were exchanged, but nobody answered until Marshal Keno's deep voice drew everybody's attention.

'You say you'd up Rapp's compensation to fifty thousand. I'll give him the chance to accept. If he refuses, he'll have to face the consequences. I'll find a way to move him.'

'Within the law?' Sam Newcombe wanted to know, his gaze resting firmly on the marshal.

Keno made an expansive gesture with both hands. 'I am the law, Mr Newcombe, elected by the townsfolk.'

There was a collective sigh of relief around the table, a surge of gratitude towards the marshal.

Floyd Cresswell poured himself another whiskey, then said, 'I propose we authorize the marshal to take appropriate action.'

Matt Warner immediately seconded the proposal.

'All in favour?' the mayor asked.

Every man sitting around the table raised his hand apart from Sam Newcombe.

'Let's be clear,' he said. 'I'm only in favour if your actions are strictly within the law.'

'Sure, Mr Newcombe,' Keno affirmed. He exchanged a meaningful nod with William Greygoose, remembering the railroad man's words. *Get that German bastard out of Coldwater Valley and the company will make sure you're a rich man. And we'll forget about certain unwholesome events in your past.*

After the meeting was finished and the courtroom locked up, Sam Newcombe walked through streets lit by gas lamps to his fine Romanesque-style house on the outskirts of town. He was proud of his home with its distinctive arched windows. He was proud of Harvest Springs too, and his ambitions for its future. As he entered, the black maid appeared, spoke a respectful greeting and took his hat. He found his wife Josephine and daughter Susan sitting in the drawing-room, busy at their embroidery.

'A good meeting, honey?' Josephine enquired.

He lowered himself into a leather-winged chair. 'Sure it was. I guess the railroad'll head this way with no problem. Harvest Springs will become a boom town, maybe even state capital.'

'How about those German folk in Coldwater Valley?' his daughter asked, turning her intense hazel eyes upon him. She had recently come back from schooling in the East, but she was well aware of local interests. 'Are they going to move out, Dad?'

Newcombe cleared his throat. 'I guess so,' he said and immediately changed the subject, enquiring about the progress of the women's embroidery, but Susan hadn't missed the slight uncertainty in his response.

Inwardly, he felt uneasy about Keno and hoped he wouldn't overstep the mark.

★ ★ ★

An explosion shattered the afternoon's calm as Helmut and Delphinia rode along the forest trails. Delphinia was dressed in shirt and jeans and rode astride, and from a distance might have been mistaken for a man. Back at the cabin, their helper, old Jack Bentley, was looking after Rosa. Now they reined in and calmed their horses.

'Railroaders must be blasting their way through some hillside,' Helmut said angrily. 'They'll ruin this country.'

Delphinia said, 'Did you ever suspect they had plans to come through our valley?'

Helmut sighed uneasily. 'I just hoped they wouldn't.' He knew inwardly that the prospect was something he hadn't wished to think about, had hoped that if he ignored it, the problem might never materialize. Now, he could do little but curse the dilemma he was in.

The Rapps had set out early that morning, intent on viewing what seemed to them like an invading army. They had crossed the great undulations of land, sweating in the day's heat. When they topped out on a valley-rim twenty minutes later, another explosion made the earth shudder and had their horses rearing in panic.

Beneath them was a scene of seething activity. Workers, some clearly Chinese in their flat coolie hats, swarmed everywhere. A great length of track had already been extended into the narrow valley, and men laboured at laying the rails and spiking them in. On the adjacent slopes was a multitude of stumps where trees had been felled for the sleepers. At the far left, graders were working with black powder, preparing another detonation to extend a tunnel through the rock. Teams of other men toiled with pickaxes, sledge-hammers and shovels, loading rocks and rubble into mule-drawn carts. To the east a great trestle bridge had been constructed, carrying the track across a gorge. This was already being put to use. A locomotive, a so-called iron horse, was approaching, clanging its bell, belching out smoke and a shower of sparks as it hauled a line of wagons laden with supplies. Telegraph lines had been erected alongside the track, and on the far side of the valley was a conglomeration of tents and a few log huts; a makeshift town, which provided accommodation for the workers.

Neither Helmut nor Delphinia could suppress a gasp at the industry spread beneath them. Helmut put his secondary fears into words, hoping that his wife would see reasons for his being against selling their land.

'Imagine if this comes through our valley, Delphinia. Everything we've known and worked for will be destroyed. Nothing will compensate us for crushing our way of life. People will come in swarms. The land will be crowded with farms, factories, houses, mines. And wherever crowds of people are, there's misery. That's why folks want to escape the big cities in the East and settle out here — but they'll bring their misery with them, you mark my words. If this is a free country as they claim, nothing should force a man to sell what he doesn't wish to.' And then he thought: *Or what he doesn't own!*

'If the railroad does come our way,' Delphinia said, 'how long will it be before it reaches us?'

Helmut smoothed his beard with an agitated hand. 'Maybe three or four weeks. Maybe less.'

Delphinia gave a perplexed nod, then

asked, 'How can you fight all those people?'

Helmut felt uneasiness squirming inside him. Now he was fully appreciating what he was up against. Eventually he opened his mouth to speak but bridled his tongue, and Delphinia concluded that the only real weapons he had were his stubbornness and his pride.

She didn't push him for further explanation. They'd both been taken aback by the sheer scale and power of the railroad. She looked at Helmut again, saw the hardened jaw, the wild glint in the eyes — and she shuddered. She had never seen such unreasonableness in him. She sensed he would not give way, not unless they killed him.

9

On their way back; the daylight faded, the bright green of leaf and grass darkening as the sun declined, leaving a twilight chill. With darkness, they halted in a forest glade and built a campfire. In different circumstances, Delphinia would have delighted in this opportunity for them to have time to themselves, but her thoughts dwelt on her daughter. She loved Rosa dearly, though the girl was becoming increasingly difficult, her physical urges and frustrations far outgrowing her simple mind.

After hobbling their horses, they made a fire, boiled coffee and ate the remains of the food Delphinia had prepared. They sat for a while, listening to the snap and spit of green sticks in the fire.

'Helmut,' she said, 'why don't we

take the money and move out?'

Helmut sat hunched, his eyes narrowed, the flames causing harlequin shadows to dance across his sombre face. He shook his head. He had no words to counter her logic.

After a long while he glanced at her and she saw in his eyes his plea for her patience and understanding. They wrapped themselves in blankets, using their saddles as pillows, lying in each other's arms.

Delphinia remained awake, gazing up through the branches at the stars, hearing the stirrings of the horses, the scurrying of wild creatures amid the fallen leaves and the ceaseless chirp of crickets. Her mind grappled with the problems ahead. How could one small family stand firm against not only the awesome might of the railroad barons, but also against the financial interests of the powerful Harvest Springs élite? Helmut had always seemed a rational man. Why had he changed?

Having no answers, she eventually

drifted into troubled sleep.

They rode through the hot morning, the sweet aroma of woodland humus rising about them, the sky a gentian blue. They approached Coldwater Valley just before noon and noticed a small white tent pitched at the base of the eastern slope, half-hidden by trees. It was the same sort of frame tent they'd seen in the railroaders' 'town'. They heeled their horses forward. Riding close to the tent, they discovered that nobody was home. The entrance flap was thrown back and on an upturned box they noticed a number of small brushes in tin cans.

'Toothbrushes!' Delphinia said.

They nudged their horses onward. They noticed how the trunks of certain trees had been blazed, then, ten minutes later, they got their first glimpse of intruders . . . about half a dozen white-shirted men, along with their mules. They seemed to be measuring the ground, working with a complicated-looking instrument on a tripod and making notes on boarded charts. They were so busy pointing and discussing aspects of the terrain that they failed to see the approaching riders.

'Railroad surveyors!' Helmut said. When they were some twenty yards away, he reined in his horse and drew his Winchester from its scabbard at his knee.

Indignation burned into him. '*Get off my land*!' he yelled.

As the startled men turned, he pressed his trigger and the boom of the gun was like thunder. Lead swooshed inches above their heads. Delphinia glimpsed their alarmed, ashen faces, saw how they gathered up their equipment and stumbled to their mules. Meanwhile, Helmut had recharged his rifle and he fired again. The surveyors didn't stop to argue, but climbed on to their mounts and heeled them away up the slope. Within minutes they had dipped beyond a ridge and there was no sign of them apart from the settling dust and the final bray of an indignant mule.

Helmut sheathed his rifle. The reverberation of the shots hung about them.

Later, after Delphinia had cooked them a meal and they had told Bentley and Rosa what they had seen, Helmut and the dog Mattie walked out to where the tent had been. The encampment was gone, including the toothbrushes. The surveyors must have dismantled the canvas and made a hasty retreat, seemingly only too willing to depart and report to their railroad bosses. But Helmut had the forlorn feeling that the surveyors might already have completed their work.

★ ★ ★

Three days later Helmut went to town to collect supplies; thankfully he was no longer required to pay his monthly visit to Ingrid, but he wanted to see her none the less. It was Saturday, mid-afternoon, and already the sound of activity came from within the saloon, the tinkling of a piano, the chinking of glasses, the shrillness of a female singer lifting her voice in competition with the rowdiness of seemingly unappreciative male voices. A big herd of Texas longhorns had pulled up at the river near Harvest Springs and the drovers had come to town in force.

Helmut parked his wagon in a side alley. He went directly to the rear of the saloon, to Ingrid's room, but there was no response to his knock. She was probably in the saloon and he had no wish to meet her there. He was disappointed. He had wanted to speak to her about the railroad's offer of compensation, to see if she would allow him some means of escape from the trap he was in.

★ ★ ★

Marshal Thomas Keno had gazed over the top of the smoke-soiled lace curtain that adorned his office window and grunted with satisfaction when he saw Helmut Rapp ride up the main street of Harvest Springs on his wagon. He had long reasoned that he would be able to prevail over Delphinia Rapp, even get her to sign a paper in the absence of her husband. He reckoned the woman's signature would be just as acceptable as her husband's. That was the way he was going to play it anyway. And once he had her signature, he'd be in a position to force the Rapps out of Coldwater Valley — all within the law, as Sam Newcombe had emphasized. Keno was determined not to become personally tainted with any high-handed activity, so he would send a couple of his deputies along to strong-arm the woman, if necessary, into signing the document Greygoose had passed to him. Anyway, he had an appointment with one of the German girls at the saloon and he felt in desperate need of womanly comforts.

He swung back into the long narrow room that was his office. Deputy Abe Mason, forty years old, was sprawled face down across his desk, snoring softly. As he slept, his right hand rested on the well-thumbed Holy Bible he was always studying. Keno gave his shoulder a rough poke and Mason spluttered awake.

'What the . . . ?' He refrained from profanity with some effort.

'Got a job for you,' Keno said. 'Take Higgins and go out to the Rapp place.'

'Thomas, that's a good fifteen miles and it's getting late in the day. No time to go disturbing folks . . . '

'You do as you're told,' Keno growled back. 'That's what you're damned well paid for.' He reached into a drawer and drew out Greygoose's document. He studied it for a moment, then reached for a pen and made an entry on it.

'Rapp is in town,' he said. 'The Rapp woman will be at home by herself, well, her and that simple-minded daughter.

Tell her that compensation has been raised to fifty thousand dollars. You get her to sign this paper accepting the offer. Once we've got her squiggle, we'll have authority to get them off the land.'

'She won't sign the paper without her husband being there.'

'She'll do the signing,' Keno explained. 'She'll do the signing if you work things right. If necessary, threaten her a bit. Maybe suggest things won't be too good for her scatty-brained daughter if she objects. Understand?'

Mason frowned. 'Sure I understand,' he said. 'And one thing's for sure. What you're suggesting ain't reasonable. We've got no right to strong-arm any woman into signing, threatening her. If you have that sort of thing in mind, Thomas, count me out.'

'Damn you, Abe,' Keno snapped. 'About time you made up your mind. Either you're a goody-goody Bible-puncher or you're a deputy marshal. You can't be both!'

Mason stood up. He had applied for

a place at a theological college in the East, and Sam Newcombe was giving him every support. Once qualified, he would come back to Harvest Springs and be minister of a new church. He had not told Keno of his plans yet, but in the meantime he had no intention of getting involved with any underhand dealings.

'I'm sorry, Thomas,' he said. 'You best get somebody else to do this job.'

It was on the tip of Keno's tongue to fire Abe Mason here and now, but he knew that Newcombe favoured the man, so, with great effort, he steadied his anger and said, 'Have it your way then, Abe. I'll get Greg Higgins and young Briggs to go out to Coldwater Valley. They won't flinch at a little work.'

Inwardly, Keno was uneasy about sending Greg Higgins without Abe Mason to 'mind' him. Higgins had a dangerous temper, taking everything as a slight. Young Briggs would hardly be able to restrain him if he flew into one of his furies, because he was scarcely more than a kid himself. But Keno considered he had no option.

*   *   *

Helmut decided to tackle his problem from a different angle. He left the saloon and walked up the street, steeling himself for some hard talking. He found the land agent's office and entered, the bell on the door bringing a youthful clerk to the desk from the back room.

'Mr Newcombe,' Helmut announced. 'I want to see him urgently.'

The clerk looked doubtful. 'Have you an appointment?'

'*Nein*! Tell him Helmut Rapp is here from Coldwater Valley. Tell him . . . ' The door from a side office was opened to reveal Sam Newcombe. He greeted Helmut with a smile and said, 'Come in. We need to talk.'

'Sure we do!' Helmut followed the town-owner into his office and a moment later was sitting in a wing-backed leather chair, had been provided with a whiskey and a fine Havana cigar. Behind Newcombe's ornate desk was a large map of the territory, and clearly etched upon it was a red line showing the proposed route of the railroad. As both men lit up, Newcombe said, 'You know the offer for your land has been increased to fifty thousand dollars? That's good money.'

Helmut snorted his contempt. 'Like I told that railroad man, I wouldn't accept the offer if it was increased to five hundred thousand dollars. I've poured so much sweat into the soil, that it's part of me now. I'll never move and I want you to divert the railroad away from my valley.'

'I can't do that, Helmut,' Newcombe commented in a soft voice. 'I wish I could, but I can't. The railroad has got to come. If it can't run through Coldwater Valley, it'll bypass Harvest Springs completely, and we'll lose our chance to become the most important stopping-place in the state. The water facilities in any other town are not adequate, and once we have the railroad the cattle drovers will come up from Texas in their thousands, bringing their herds in. You're a far-sighted man, Helmut. Can't you see how the population is crying out for prosperity and progress, and that's what the railroad is all about? We need it to bind the country together. It'll make us all rich. You as much as anybody else.'

'Me and my Delphinia are rich already, Mr Newcombe. Not with money, but with our freedom. We don't want gold. We've got what we want — the land, the peacefulness, the good clean air. The railroad will bring trouble and misery, you mark my words.'

Newcombe was shaking his head in disagreement. Much of the good humour had drained from his face. Greygoose had described this man as stubborn and by golly he was right. Newcombe tried to keep his impatience from showing.

'One thing's certain, Helmut. One way or another, the railroad *will* come through Coldwater Valley. The odds against you are too strong. You're not big enough to stop progress being made. But I promise you that I'll do everything I can to relocate you somewhere that will be just as fine as Coldwater Valley, maybe better. I'll make sure you get more than adequate compensation for your land, and the best building materials on the market to establish a new home. You'll have everything you need, and more. I can't be fairer than that!'

Helmut drummed his fingers in a harsh tattoo on the arm of his chair. He wondered what Newcombe's reaction would be if he knew that the land was not his to sell, that any compensation would go straight into the pocket of Ingrid, or Abigail as she now called herself. Helmut was in a cleft stick and he could see no way out. All he could do was stand his ground. His words came unwaveringly, not loud-spoken but with an intensity that appeared to leave not the slightest margin for doubt.

'We are not giving up our land, no matter what you offer. You'll have to kill us to get us out of the way. I'll promise that on the Bible if you wish.'

He drained his whiskey and rapped the glass on to the desktop. Frustration burned into him. He rose to his feet. 'There's no point in us wasting any more time, Mr Newcombe. I can see that. Thank you for the whiskey. Good day to you.' And he spun on his heel and left the office.

He walked to the saloon, went inside and ordered a beer. As he stood at the bar a man with a vaguely familiar face said, 'You look as mad as a peeled rattler.'

'I feel that way,' Helmut retorted. 'Those railroaders have no right bullying me out of my land. I wish I could blast the whole lot of them back where they came from.'

10

Delphinia Rapp always felt lonely and vulnerable at the homestead when Helmut was away. She stepped out on to the porch, hand raised to shade her eyes against the last blaze of the sun as it sank behind the mountains. The air was quiet and windless. She had grown used to the silence of the land, but this evening the hush seemed extra eerie and funereal. Even the birds had quieted. Suddenly the shrill laughter of Rosa sounded. The girl was hidden from view, down in the chicken-coop, as so often, with her beloved birds. Delphinia sighed, forever perplexed by her daughter.

She was turning back inside, when the distant snort of a horse caught her attention, and her heart briefly lifted as she wondered if Helmut was returning, but then she realized it would probably be some hours before he got back. She strained her eyes into the distance and spotted the movement of two horsemen approaching through the shadows along the valley side. As they drew closer, she could see nothing familiar about them and she concluded that they were strangers. She wondered if they were from the railroad, maybe more of those surveyors. Her uneasiness deepened. As she stepped back into the room, her glance lifted to the heavy Winchester on the wall. Helmut had made sure that it was always loaded and ready, ever since the visit of Marshal Keno and the railroad man Greygoose. She thought of Rosa. She returned to the porch and called to her and soon the girl appeared, trudging reluctantly up to the cabin.

'What is it, Ma?' she inquired.

'Riders are coming in. I don't know who they are. We'd better be careful. Stay close.'

The girl nodded vaguely, but her interest sharpened as she joined her mother and peered at the approaching strangers. They were getting nearer. She noticed that both of them were quite young. The second rider attracted her gaze particularly. He had wide shoulders and flowing hair-locks.

Realizing that they were observed, the foremost man raised his arm in greeting and a moment later they drew rein in the cabin yard and slipped from their animals. He looked about twenty, with a habit of constantly widening his eyes, sometimes grinning to reveal jagged teeth. The grin faded as quickly as it appeared, and his presence immediately discomforted Delphinia.

'The name's Higgins. I'm Deputy over at Harvest Springs.' He nodded to his companion. 'This here is my sidekick, Joe Briggs. We been sent by the marshal to explain things to you. Is your husband around?' He cocked his head, feigning disappointment when the woman stated that Helmut was in town.

Rosa was not listening to the conversation. She was too busy exchanging coy glances with young Briggs. He had a round face that seemed almost too youthful to support the scrabble of moustache and the silky stubble that decorated his jaw, and somehow this made him more fascinating to Rosa. His long hair was the colour of yellow corn.

Briggs acknowledged the way she felt by smiling approvingly as he let his eyes rake over the ripeness of her body. The sight of her ivory skin, and the way the calico dress was only casually fastened did nothing to hide the fullness of her curves. How he would love to pop those buttons undone and explore what was beneath, her breasts and the softness of her belly! He figured her nipples would be pale and soft. He swallowed hard and groaned, his heartbeat quickening.

The customary urge to show hospitality to travellers caused a welcome to rise to Delphinia's lips, though inwardly she felt wary of these men. 'You'd better come in. I'll get you a bite of supper.'

'Well, that's right kindly, Mrs Rapp.'

The visitors stepped up on to the porch and into the cabin and were soon seated at the table, their sweaty smell filling the room. They wolfed back the victuals Delphinia laid before them — cold slices of pork, bread, apple pie and a jug of fresh creamy milk. They ate as if they had not had a meal for days, then came back for seconds. Delphinia lit an oil-lamp for the night had slipped in; her hand had trembled slightly as she tore a match from its block and Higgins had noticed and grinned.

Rosa stood watching. She couldn't take her eyes off young Briggs.

'Can I take Joe to see my chickens?' she asked her mother.

'No, honey. You just stay where you are and be a good girl.'

Rosa unleashed a dramatic sigh.

Greg Higgins finished his apple pie and wiped the crumbs from his moustache with the back of his hand.

'We come on business, Mrs Rapp,' he said. 'Of course we would've liked your husband to be here, but I'm sure you'll do just as well. We've come to make an offer, authorized by the Town Committee of Harvest Springs, to increase the compensation for moving out of this valley to fifty thousand dollars.'

The mention of the money momentarily drew Rosa's attention away from young Briggs. Her eyes were shining as she said, 'Oh Ma. Just think how we could spend all that money. New dresses, hats, pretty scarves and — '

'Be quiet, Rosa!' her mother snapped.

Rosa lowered her eyes sulkily, then swung her attention back to Joe Briggs.

'She's sure right,' Greg Higgins grinned, 'it's an offer nobody could refuse. You'll be wealthy folk.' He dragged the formal document from his pocket, unfolded it and laid it upon the table in front of Delphinia. 'Of course normally we'd want your husband to sign, but if you'd be good enough to do the necessary, I'm sure it'll do just as well and then we needn't detain you any longer.'

Delphinia eyed the formally written words: *I, Delphinia Rapp, hereby agree the sale of Coldwater Valley, to the M. & P.C. Railroad Company for the sum of $50,000 . . .*

'How come,' she said suspiciously, 'that if you were expecting to see my husband, this form is already made out in my name?'

Higgins coughed, hesitated, and said, 'Like I said, everybody will be quite happy with your signature, you being an educated lady.'

'Helmut wouldn't be happy,' Delphinia cried, anger flaring in her green eyes. 'He says he'll never sell this land!'

'Oh, Mrs Rapp, you won't get a better offer than this. I'm sure your husband will be delighted with the deal.'

'I won't sign,' Delphinia said firmly, 'and that's that. Now, unless there's anything else to discuss, perhaps you'll leave us in peace.'

Higgins's threadbare patience snapped. He banged both his palms down upon the table and stood up, his eyes widening with frightening intensity. Suddenly Rosa's voice cut across him.

'Ma, I'm just going down to see the chickens.'

'No, Rosa,' Delphinia retorted. 'It's dark now.'

But the girl took no notice and walked on out through the open doorway.

'Now think again,' Higgins demanded menacingly. 'Fifty thousand dollars is a fortune in anybody's eyes, and all you have to do is sign this damned paper and it's yours.' Delphinia bit her lower lip in exasperation. She did not like the man cursing in front of her. Sure enough what they were offering was big money, but she knew full well what Helmut's reaction would be. *Nein, nein, nein!*

She shook her head. 'I'll never sign anything unless my husband's here.

He's head of this household, not me.'

Higgins widened his eyes. 'Mrs Rapp, don't make me angry!'

Delphinia was about to respond when she realized that not only had Rosa gone outside into the night, but so had Higgins's corn-haired companion, Joe Briggs — and suddenly a flush of panic went through her. What was going on? Rosa was so naïve, so vulnerable . . . and he was a young, horny man . . . She shuddered.

She faced Higgins squarely and her words came with grit. 'Get it into your thick skull, mister, if anybody signs that paper, it will be my husband, not me — '

'Mrs Rapp, you better sign that paper. It'll be best for you . . . *and the girl*!' She felt the spray of his spit on her face. She figured he was the ugliest man she had ever seen.

It was then that Rosa's scream came from the outside, slicing through the night like the cry of a banshee.

'Oh God!' Delphinia cried.

Higgins snatched up the paper and spun on his heel, leaving the cabin, striding out into the night. Delphinia rushed across the room and lifted the heavy Winchester down from its pegs. Then she hurried after Higgins. *What were they doing to Rosa?*

Delphinia's heart was pounding. Everywhere was gloomy, the stars not yet having pierced the clouds. Suddenly she heard the thud of hoofs and she saw the shadowy scurrying of movement across the yard. She realized that her two unwelcome visitors were leaving. A fleeting feeling of relief swept through her, but when she cried out 'Rosa! Rosa!', listened for a response and none came, her terror returned. This was a nightmare she should never have allowed to happen.

She ran down to the chicken-coop, calling again and again. Pantingly, she peered about, cursing the gloom, making the birds cluck indignantly, but soon she realized that Rosa was not here. Keno had hinted that Rosa might suffer if the Rapps resisted the railroad's plans. *Oh my God!* She had always suspected he meant what he said. The men must have taken Rosa.

Delphinia unleashed a yowl.

Half stumbling, she hurried back into the cabin, tried to stem the tremble in her hands, fumbled with the matches and lit a lantern. *Be calm*, she told herself, *you'll gain nothing by panicking*, but she could not suppress her emotions. She hastened to the barn where their sorrel horse was stabled. The beast sensed the fear in her. It snorted and stamped its feet, showing the whites of its eyes. Somehow she got the bridle fitted, a saddle across its back, and drew the cinch tight. She had left the heavy gun leaning against the wall. Now she recovered it, hoisted up her skirts, got her foot into the stirrup and dragged herself astride the saddle. Slamming with her heels, she urged the sorrel out of the barn, feeling sure the men would be heading back for town. She gave the horse its head, and it needed no encouragement to stretch into a pounding gallop. She prayed that Rosa had not been violated, or worse — and felt her own guilt for not properly protecting her daughter.

As she rode, fear fluttered like wings in her stomach. Ten minutes later, she drew up in frustration, convinced she had lost the other riders. Maybe they had drawn off the trail, maybe . . . She swung round, desperation bringing a wail of despair from her. She drove the horse more slowly now, straining her ears for any sound. And at last the sound came to her — men's laughter, whooping riotous yells of mirth and encouragement, coming from back in the trees.

Then she heard Rosa scream again.

She reined in and half fell from the saddle, struggling with her long skirt. In her haste, she lost her grip on the gun and it clattered down, thankfully not going off. She gathered it up and ran towards the apparent source of the sounds. The moon had now lifted, sending its shafts of silver down through the tree fronds. Rising above the frantic rasp of her breathing, she heard Rosa groaning and then the angry shout of a man — Joe Briggs! Suddenly she saw the girl running up the slope ahead, darting through the trees like a terrified nymph. Briggs was stumbling after her, unleashing a string of obscenities.

Delphinia halted, lifted the Winchester into her shoulder and tried to steady it. She could not, it was so heavy and she was trembling with agitation, but she pressed the trigger and the gun's roar filled the night with an awesome blast, setting her ears singing. She peered into the gloom, breathing in the smell of gunpowder, momentarily blinded by the spurt of flame that the detonation had created. She dropped the gun, this time intentionally, ran forward and nigh stumbled over the body of Joe Briggs sprawled face down on the ground. She gasped, crouched down. He was deathly still, a crumpled unmoving hulk — and in the moonlight she saw the glint of his blood.

Instinct told her that he was dead. But her concern centred on Rosa and she straightened up and struggled in the direction she had last glimpsed her terrified daughter. Soon she heard the girl's mournful sobs. She found her slumped on the ground, her face buried in her hands. She flinched as Delphinia knelt beside her, no doubt fearing that it was Briggs, but she relaxed as her mother hugged her, soothing her. Delphinia thanked God that she had her back, maternal instinct blinding her to all else.

'What happened, my love?' she murmured. 'What did they do to you?'

But her daughter did not answer, just sobbed mournfully, her tears soaking into Delphinia's dress.

Presently, she helped Rosa to her feet, noting how her dress was torn and crumpled. The sorrel stood patiently as she pulled herself into the saddle and then, with new-found strength, she hoisted the girl up behind her. Delphinia paid no heed to the dead man, nor his companion, wherever he was, but heeled the sorrel back towards the cabin.

Only when they were home, and Delphinia had done her best to calm her daughter and tucked her safely into bed, did the full gravity of what had happened sink into her brain. She pressed her hands over her ears. She could hear her blood pounding through her veins. She could also hear the voice crying out inside her.

I killed a man. Oh God!

11

When Helmut eventually reached home, he found Delphinia slumped over the table, the lantern burned low. She was so strung up and tearful that it took him an age to discover what had happened.

'You were defending the girl?' he eventually said, trying to settle things in his own mind.

Delphinia lifted her tearful face and nodded.

'Then what you did was right,' he went on. 'No telling what he would have done to her. Maybe he'd already . . . Rosa must tell us.'

But Rosa lay rigid in her bed, staring at the ceiling, and no matter how hard they questioned her, she did nothing but sob. Helmut took her in his arms, trying to comfort his little rose, but not a single coherent word could they get from her and finally he rested her back down and they left her and returned to the cabin's main room.

'Well,' Helmut said, slipping his arm around his wife's shoulder, 'we shall have to wait and see what happens. But if you were defending Rosa, my love, you did right. You only did what any mother would have done.'

'I never meant to kill him,' Delphinia whispered.

After a moment Helmut said, 'We'd best ride out and see if the body's still there. We'll go first thing in the morning.'

The suggestion seemed to startle Delphinia. She raised her face, horrified, but after a second she gave a resigned nod.

They were awake long before dawn. Everything seemed stark and cold and damp until Helmut got the stove started. Rosa still did not speak and Helmut wondered if she would ever again utter words. She moved around like a zombie, not eating breakfast, only her startled eyes reflecting emotion.

Helmut had the forlorn feeling that she hardly recognized them. She just moped, adding to the general misery.

As the first glimmer of ghost-light fingered the valley rim, Helmut and Delphinia rode out from the cabin, intent on seeing if the body was still where it had fallen. It took them some twenty minutes to reach the spot. They dismounted and tethered their horses, and then Delphinia led the way through the trees to a clearing and gazed around with desperate eyes.

'It was here,' she declared.

Helmut searched about. Soon he found blood upon the ground. 'Well, the body's gone,' he said. 'Maybe you just wounded him.'

Delphinia shook her head. 'I killed him.'

Helmut came to her, took her in his arms. 'Like I said,' he murmured, 'you only did what any mother would've done.'

'But not everybody will see it that way,' Delphinia argued.

Helmut hugged his wife close, smoothing her back, but he could find no further words to console her.

After a moment they remounted their horses and rode slowly back to the cabin, not talking, both pondering on the grimness of the future.

The day dragged intolerably, hot and dusty. They tried to act normally, going about their everyday tasks, but gloom hung upon them like a shroud, and all the time Rosa gazed at her parents, her eyes mournful, her lips clamped shut in dreadful silence.

Mid-afternoon, their fears took on reality. A posse of six riders entered the valley, led by Marshal Thomas Keno. Riding alongside him was Greg Higgins. As they drew rein in the cabin yard, their faces were grim.

'I'm sure sorry about this, Helmut,' Keno said, leaning forward on his mount, easing the weight on his buttocks, 'but Deputy Joe Briggs was shot dead last night while he was carrying out his duty. Greg, here, saw it happen. There was nothing he could do. He saw Mrs Rapp shoot the boy down . . . '

'She was protecting our daughter,' Helmut cried. 'That young Briggs had done awful things to her . . . '

'That's not the way Greg told it,' Keno countered. He turned to Higgins and said, 'You tell Helmut how it happened.'

Higgins coughed, then said, 'That girl wouldn't leave Joe alone. She kept pestering him, tried to undo his shirt, would have had all the clothes off him if she'd had her way. I never seen a female so randy. She followed us as we left the cabin, and we started to get worried about her, being out in the night and all that. So we stopped and let her catch us up. She started to pester poor Joe. All he wanted to do was help her, telling her to go home. That's when Mrs Rapp rode up and started shouting. I was a few yards ahead when she fired her gun. Young Joe never stood a chance. I stayed where I was. I figured if I interfered, she'd shoot me too. Thank God she didn't see me. She was like a crazy woman. After she had taken the girl away, I went to poor Joe. He was stone dead. Died instantly, I guess. I took his body back to town.'

'*Nein!*' Helmut exclaimed. 'It wasn't like that.'

Another man in the posse said, 'Well, let the girl talk. She'll tell what happened.'

'Rosa's been struck dumb,' Helmut explained. 'She's not said a word since last night.'

There was a moment's silence while Helmut's words were digested, then Keno spoke.

'Mr Helmut, I got no alternative but to take your wife in on a charge of murder. She'll get a fair trial, that's for sure, but she'll have to face justice.'

'You'll not take her,' Helmut said firmly. 'I'll not allow it!'

But suddenly Delphinia's voice came. She had stepped on to the porch, drawing a shawl about her shoulders.

'I'll go with them. There's been enough trouble already.'

Helmut drew a shuddering breath. 'Delphinia, you can't . . .'

'Yes I can,' she stated. 'If I face a judge, I'll explain exactly what happened, how we've been pressured to move out of this valley. How they tried to get me to sign that paper.'

Helmut emitted a low growling sound, knowing he was helpless to prevent his wife's arrest.

Rosa had stayed in her room, too frightened to emerge.

Helmut reluctantly made a decision. 'So be it then. And I just hope justice will prevail. Delphinia's a good woman and mother, kind and loving. She's no killer. But if she's to be taken to town, then you've got to look after her properly. She has got to be treated like the lady she is. Do you understand?'

Keno said, 'She'll be treated fair. You can visit her tomorrow and see we've done right by her.'

Helmut said, 'Will you ask Jack Bentley to come over tomorrow and look after the girl while I come to town?'

Keno nodded.

A moment later Helmut was saddling a horse, working with heavy hands and a heavier heart. Meanwhile, Delphinia gathered together the few necessary things that any woman would need. Before she left the cabin, she gave Rosa a hug and a kiss and told her not to wander from the cabin or cause her father trouble, and that they were to make sure to eat properly, but her daughter only looked at her vaguely and did not understand what was happening. Outside, Keno and the men of the posse waited, their expressions showing impatience. Helmut held his wife in his arms, but he was too choked to say the things he should have done. She did not speak either, but gave him a tight hug and when she drew back her face was shining with tears. Helmut helped her up into her saddle.

'You got that ointment for the burn on your face?' he enquired, and she nodded, then he whispered, 'I love you, always will.'

When they were ready, Keno waved them forward, a cynical smile touching his lips, and Helmut stood watching as the riders moved away down the valley, the dust rising behind them, the horses' hoofs giving a hollow scrape against the ground. Eventually they crossed over the rim and were gone.

Helmut went inside, found Rosa and said, 'Why didn't you speak up? Why didn't you tell them what Joe Briggs was doing to you? Why didn't you tell them what really happened?'

She just stared at him, her face expressionless, her lips shut tight.

'I reckon you could talk if you had to,' he shouted, and then he was ashamed of himself for he had never before raised his voice to her.

For the rest of the day and evening, he busied himself about the homestead, seeing to the hogs, the cow and chickens, chopping some kindling for the stove and later on cooking supper. Finally he worked at braiding a new reata from strings of thin rawhide.

Sometimes he gazed off into the distance, hoping that Delphinia would appear, having sorted everything out. She didn't come. Rosa sauntered off to the chicken-coop, but he kept an eye on her, making sure she didn't wander further. The last thing he wanted was for her to disappear.

Dusk brought its special brand of silence. He reckoned Delphinia would be lodged in the town's jail by now. It didn't seem possible . . . his dear wife behind bars! The whole world had gone crazy. What would happen to her?

Unless Rosa found her tongue, which he doubted, it would be Delphinia's word against Greg Higgins's; he claimed he had seen everything. Furthermore, Higgins was a deputy marshal and doubtless a friend of Keno's and other important folk in town. His word would be more readily accepted than that of an out-of-town woman who was hardly known in Harvest Springs. What would they do to a woman found guilty of murder?

And then, somehow, his mind swung to the railroad, by now creeping ever closer like some evil serpent. How could he resist its advance? So many of his problems would have remained dormant but for the greed of men who wanted to exploit this country.

When darkness came he called to Rosa and they ate supper in silence, she watching him with her big eyes. Afterwards, he made sure she went to bed and he cleared the dishes and presently sat at the table, pondering on things. He kept thinking about Delphinia. She didn't deserve what was happening to her. All she'd ever really cared about was her family, making sure they were safe and loved. And she had always been so proud of him and their marriage. His eyes moistened as he rested his head down upon his arms and things got muddled in his mind. His life was in a shambles. Sunk in depression at his own weakness, he drifted into sleep there in the chair, the dog Mattie curled close to his leg.

12

The cock-crow awakened him. He felt stiff and unrested and he forced himself up, his brain gradually taking hold of the events of the previous day. He poured some water into a basin and freshened his face, then, taking a bucket, he went down to the barn and milked the cow. He let the hogs out to rummage in the meadow and collected four newly laid eggs from the chicken-coop. When he returned to the cabin Rosa had risen from her bed. He cooked some bacon for breakfast, wishing that his daughter would do something to help with the chores, but she did nothing. And yet he couldn't be hard on her. It wasn't her fault that her brain was not sound.

At noon he spotted a rider coming down the valley and realized it was Jack Bentley, come to look after Rosa while he was away. The old man dismounted stiffly, cursing his rheumatism, then he reached out and grasped Helmut's hand.

'I heard Delphinia's going to stand trial,' he said. 'Higgins swears blind that it was a cold-blooded act and that Joe Briggs had done nothing to Rosa to warrant his killing. Briggs's family have gone crazy, saying what a good upright son Joe was, that he'd never hurt a fly and vowing to see his killer hung!'

'Hung!' The word escaped Helmut's lips like an oath. He gave his head a despairing shake. 'I don't know.' He plunged his bearded face into his hands. After a moment he recovered and they went back into the cabin. He took Rosa in his arms. At this moment it seemed she was all he had left. He gazed into her face, told her how her papa loved her, but she showed no emotion.

* * *

That afternoon, Delphinia sat in her cell. Her throat ached with misery, but her eyes were dry, as if they could never be moistened with tears again. She knew that there were so many chores to be done at home and here was she, frustrated and wretched in a cage. The jangle of keys intruded into her thoughts and one of the deputies, a new man called Denton, said, 'A visitor for you, Mrs Rapp.'

Delphinia looked up to see a young, fresh-faced woman entering the cell. She wore a good calico dress, a bonnet, and carried a pair of gloves.

'I'm Susan Newcombe,' she announced. 'Sam Newcombe's daughter. I've brought you some home cooking, a few books and an embroidery pattern with wools. I do hope they will comfort you.'

Delphinia realized here was a bright, sensitive girl who was deeply saddened by what had happened. She sat up, straightening her hair. 'It's truly kind of you.'

Susan sat down alongside Delphinia

on the cell's hard wooden bench, settling herself without the least formality. 'My dad's really sorry about what's happened,' she said. 'He never wanted trouble like this. None of us did.'

'But he wants the railroad to come?' Delphinia said.

Susan gave her head a pert nod. 'The whole town wants the railroad to come, and it's impossible to prevent so many people from getting what they want. And, Mrs Rapp, Dad says he'll pay for you to get proper legal representation.'

Delphinia frowned. 'It'll do no good. You see, I've no defence. I shot him, I can't deny that.'

'But you didn't mean to kill him,' Susan prompted.

Delphinia rubbed her face with her hands. 'I don't know. I didn't think. I don't know what came over me. I just didn't want Rosa to get hurt.'

'But Greg Higgins says Joe Briggs had no intention of hurting Rosa.'

'I don't think that's true,' Delphinia said.

'But can't she tell us what happened?' Susan Newcombe asked.

Delphinia shook her head. 'She's either struck dumb or playing dumb, who can tell? Maybe one day her tongue will come back and she'll tell the truth.'

'A good lawyer will make sure the truth comes out,' Susan said, but a look of hopelessness had settled over Delphinia.

At that moment both women heard the scuffle of activity from the outer office and Deputy Denton unlocked the cell door again. 'You're doing well for visitors today, Mrs Rapp.'

Helmut appeared and Delphinia rose to embrace him, then she said, 'Susan Newcombe kindly brought me some things.'

Helmut extended his hand and Susan shook it. The girl was elegant and had a kind smile which warmed him. He could smell the sweet perfume she wore. 'Pleased to meet you, Miss Newcombe.'

'Oh, call me Susan,' she said. 'I must be on my way. I'll come again, Mrs Rapp, if you don't mind. Anything I can do to help, do let me know.'

Delphinia expressed her gratitude, truly moved by the girl's thoughtfulness, but then it occurred to her that here was the daughter of the man who was behind so much of their troubles. Had it not been for Sam Newcombe, the town of Harvest Springs would never have been created, the railroad would never have come this way and Coldwater Valley would have remained the peaceful haven that it had been when first the Rapps had built their homestead. But none of this showed in her face as she nodded farewell.

'How are you coping at home?' Delphinia asked Helmut. 'I've been so worried about you.'

Helmut forced himself to smile. 'I'm doing fine, honey. Just missing you a lot.' And he seated himself on the bunk and did his utmost to lift his wife's spirits, though inside he felt utterly sick.

★ ★ ★

It was the following Sunday. The blasting of the tunnel that Helmut and Delphinia had observed was completed, the railroad lines had been laid through it and tracks were running into the canyon beyond. The workers had erected a new, tented camp here and, today being the Sabbath, had taken their day of rest. Some of the Chinese workers, brought in from San Francisco, did not share the Christian faith and were forced to curb their apparently boundless vigour. It seemed there was no such word as laziness in the Chinese language. To pass the time they smoked opium. Several temporary log shelters had been erected, cooks had set up their stoves and the locomotive had brought fresh supplies through the tunnel. The camp buzzed with a mixture of voices from the cosmopolitan crew — Irish, Scandinavian, Chinese, English and American. Many were former soldiers, both Union and Confederate, men who had caught the wanderlust during the Civil War; some were immigrants, flocking from poverty in the East and thankful for work; some were men on the run from the law, working under false names and glad of the anonymity offered by an employer who did not ask too many questions.

At dusk, the camp lapsed into a silence broken only by the soft notes of somebody playing a squeeze-box. Presently stars pin-pricked the heavens, fires died low, and the squeeze-box faded.

It was then that the explosion erupted.

Into its echo, men shouted in alarm as they stumbled from their tents.

Close to the tunnel entrance, Irishman Dan Fulcher had been standing guard over a heap of supplies, more asleep than awake. The explosion shook him to wakefulness. Too late he heard the cascade of rocks from above him. Stumbling away, he had no chance of avoiding the avalanche. He was felled and crushed as boulders rained down from the cliff top.

The camp had now come fully to life, voices raised in consternation. Lanterns flared and men stood gaping as the dust settled, then gingerly went forward, fearful of further explosions. At first it was suspected that a ghastly accident had occurred, that somehow, the supplies of black powder had fired off. But then as the cliff top was investigated, it became evident that it had not been an accident but an act of sabotage on the railroad. A line of boulders had been dragged into position at the very edge of the cliff, had been positioned to plunge downward when explosives were set off, blocking the newly created tunnel below, smashing the rails, destroying the progress that hard toil by the workers had won over the last few days.

John Evans, the construction chief, watched, his face showing angry-red in the flare of the lantern, as the crushed body of Dan Fulcher was extracted from beneath the rocks. Fulcher had been a popular man and a good worker, and fury was evident amongst the crowding workers against whoever had caused his death.

John Evans cursed the time that would be lost by the damage. The locomotive was trapped on the wrong side of the blocked tunnel.

'Who the hell would have done this?' he demanded. 'Everybody wants the railroad to come through.'

One of the surveyors stepped forward. 'Not everybody,' he said fervently, and he was recalling the way his party had been chased out of Coldwater Valley, the crash of shots in their ears. 'There is somebody who would do anything to stop us.'

13

The following day brought a further shock for Helmut. Old Jack Bentley rode over from Harvest Springs, his expression downcast.

After he had put his horse to pasture, he said, 'Delphinia's been taken to Leavenworth. She'll stand trial there. They reckon the case is too big for them to handle in Harvest Springs. If she's found guilty, she'd maybe get a jail sentence. They wouldn't hang a woman, Helmut.'

Helmut removed his hat. He was not so sure. He wiped the sweat from his brow with the sleeve of his coat, his expression utterly bleak. With Delphinia far away in Leavenworth, he would be even less able to help her.

As they sat down to eat, Bentley delivered more news. 'There's talk in town about an explosion out at the railroad camp. A fella was killed. Some of the track was blown up and a tunnel caved in, trapping a locomotive.'

'Who do they reckon did it?' Helmut enquired.

'I don't know, but it will only set them back a week or so.'

'Wish it could have set them back for ever,' Helmut said.

Bentley gave him an odd look, but said nothing. He knew that in town they were saying that Helmut had set off those explosives because everybody else was in favour of the railroad coming. He figured that Helmut was so against it, he might well have done a crazy deed like that.

* * *

Jack Bentley stayed at the homestead that night. Helmut was glad enough for his company, feeling totally melancholy himself. After ensuring that Rosa was safely in bed, he and his old friend sat at the table and opened a bottle of whiskey, but, despite the liquor, conversation did not come easily; they were both too concerned about Delphinia. Eventually they went to their blankets.

Bentley's soft snoring soon sounded from the main room where he had bedded down, but Helmut lay awake. Several times he heard the restless stirrings of Rosa, and presently her low moaning came as she lapsed into slumber. He wondered what dreams were tormenting her. He wished he could communicate with her, but it seemed a barrier had arisen, encasing what was going on inside her head.

He could not escape the feeling that whatever had happened, worse was to follow. He listened to the wind's bluster snatching at the roof of the cabin, rattling in the eaves. What thoughts were tormenting Delphinia at this time?

It was after he had dozed off that a strange thing happened.

He came awake with an unpleasant suddenness, feeling cold sweat pricking his body, hearing the voice speaking with incredible clarity. It was Rosa, calling to her mother. He cast aside his blanket, slid from the bed. He struck a match and touched it to the wick of a lantern. In its light he moved to the doorway of the girl's room. To his surprise, she was sitting up on her bed, her big eyes wide.

'You got your voice back?' he gasped, but she made no response, just gazed at him, her lips drawn back, her clenched teeth showing white against the shadows of her face.

'You spoke, Rosa,' Helmut repeated. 'You spoke real words. You can tell us what happened now. You . . . ' But he trailed off as he realized that his daughter had raised her arm, was pointing over his shoulder and through the doorway to the outside window beyond. Helmut swung round, following her indication — and it was then he saw the pinpoint of light showing from across the valley. There was something unworldly about it, like a remote, evil star, fallen from the heavens.

'What the hell?' It was Jack Bentley's voice. He had risen from his blankets to stand next to Helmut. In order to see more clearly, Helmut stifled his lantern and they moved to the window, their attention riveted through the glass pane.

'We got visitors,' Helmut at last stated. He realized that what they saw was the bobbing movement of a flaming brand, held high by somebody walking over uneven ground towards the cabin, and as the light came nearer he saw that it was backed by the shadowy, relentless progress of walking figures, a whole mob of them. Soon the whooping riotous yelling of many voices wafted on the wind.

Helmut cleared his throat, shrugging off his uncertainty, trying to think clearly.

'Rosa, hide under your bed,' he commanded, but he was conscious that she made no move.

'That's a gang of railroad workers,' Jack Bentley gasped. 'They sound as if they're liquored up, and they ain't come here for a social visit!'

'But why . . . ?'

'I reckon they're blaming you, Helmut, for the explosion, for killing that worker.'

'But I never had anything to do with it,' Helmut said.

'They won't listen to reason,' Bentley grunted, agitation bringing an edge to his voice, 'and they're getting closer!'

Helmut growled with anger. He had done enough wrong in his life without getting blamed for something of which he was innocent.

He turned to Bentley. 'Jack, this trouble's got nothing to do with you. There's no cause for you to get involved. I want you to do me a favour. Take Rosa into town where she'll be safe. Hand her over to Ingrid at the Buckthorn Saloon and tell her what's — '

'Ingrid?' Bentley interrupted.

'Abigail, as she now calls herself.'

'But she's a — '

'For God's sake, there's no time for explanations. Just take her and go.'

'But I can't leave you — '

'Jack,' Helmut roared, 'go!'

Bentley cursed, but he turned, grabbed Rosa's hand and pulled her from her bed. He drew a blanket about her shoulders and lifted her in his arms.

'I don't like this,' he said, but he went out through the back of the cabin, and a moment later Helmut heard the snorting of a horse, followed by the pounding of receding hoofs. It was then that the crackle of gunfire erupted.

Helmut flung open the front door of the cabin and gazed out into the night. He could see movement in plenty. There were more burning torches now, lighting up the scurry of many men — and all at once he realized what they were about. They were shooting down his cattle. Simultaneously, a flaming torch curved through the air, landing squarely on the roof of his stable. Within seconds, flames were shooting up from the place and he heard the

157

terrified whinnying of his three horses inside.

Fury seized him, blinding him to any fear for his own safety. He charged out and across the yard to the barn. Everything was in nightmarish turmoil, ghoul-like figures flitting through his outbuildings. He heard the squeal of hogs. More torches were raining out of the sky; one descended on the roof of the cabin, setting it alight, others bounced off. Helmut reached the barn, thrust himself inside. Stumbling through the straw, he opened up the stalls, freed two of his animals, sent them stampeding out through the main door. He freed the third horse, his big sorrel, plunged his fingers into its mane and dragged himself on to its back, fighting for control as it reared up. The barn was thick with smoke, causing him to cough. A section of blazing rafters fell about his shoulders, bounced off, showering him with sparks. He rammed his heels into the sorrel's flanks. The horse squealed in rage, then went surging to the outside, colliding in the process with one of the attackers. The man was hurled away, while Helmut, clinging like a fly, pounded on.

Without saddle or bridle, he had little control and the horse bolted through smoke into a crowd of shouting men. Helmut had a brief vision of their alarmed faces turned up towards him, then the sorrel thudded amidst them, staggering as they were thrown aside. Bedlam was everywhere. He glimpsed the dark shapes of his hogs, stampeding away in front of him. Meanwhile, sparks filled the air, scorching his face, and glancing to his left he saw the cabin, a roaring mass of flame spiralling into the sky, the wind drawing smoke across the yard and outbuildings. He screamed with anguish. All he had worked for was ruined! Thank God that Bentley had got Rosa away. And thank God that Delphinia was safe from this earthly hell.

On the far side of the valley, as the incline grew rugged, Helmut lost his grip on the sorrel's mane and he slipped from its back, hitting the ground so hard that he was stunned. He lay for a while, his senses cobbled, then he forced himself up, fighting off dizziness.

The clamour from behind him had diminished, though flames were still roaring skyward from the buildings, and in the orange light they created, he could see the scattered hulks of his cows, lying where they had been shot down. The scene brought tears of chagrin to his eyes.

Barefooted, still in his nightshirt, he ran back down the slope towards the pyre that had once been his home. He stumbled over something soft and, feeling downward, he discovered it was his dog, Mattie, a bullet through her head. He rose, staggered on. The ground singed his feet. He was aware that the men who had done this awful thing were gone, disappearing into the night more quickly than they had arrived. He swore that they must be made to pay for their crime. Not even the mighty railroad could be allowed to flout the law.

He tripped and collapsed. He felt all his strength had left him. He knew there was nothing he could do to save his homestead and he wept.

14

When dawn eventually streaked the sky, he roused himself from the doze into which he had slumped. His body ached, and there was heaviness in his limbs. The whole scene was stretched before him — the gutted cabin, with only its stone chimney surviving the conflagration; the barn, the hog-pen, the chicken-coop, even the privy, were just ash, with the redness still smouldering. Gritty smoke hung in the air. He could feel it in his nostrils and throat. The bloated bodies of his cows were sprawled in the grass, already attracting buzzards. Everything he had owned, except for the nightshirt on his back, was gone.

His will and strength returned and he forced himself on to his uncertain legs. He shivered, trying to determine what he should do. His thoughts swung to

Rosa. Had Jack Bentley got her to town safely? Had Ingrid softened her heart to take her in? He had to find out. He also needed to report to the law what had happened. Thomas Keno must be made to earn his wages and justify the badge he wore.

His horses had vanished, thankfully saved from the flames. It was fifteen miles to Harvest Springs. All he had were his bare feet to carry him there, but he set out, the new day taking hold as he stumbled along, his mind numbed with grief. But fate was not altogether unkind to him; it had done him enough harm already. After two hours, a man on a wagon overtook him, carrying stock into town, and gratefully Helmut climbed up beside him. Hardly aware of what he was saying, he mumbled a response to the stranger's enquiries, somehow satisfying his curiosity.

The town was stirring into life as the wagon rolled up Main Street. Helmut expressed his gratitude to his companion and clambered down. He was desperate to confirm that Rosa was safe. Avoiding passers-by, he made his way to the rear of the Buckthorn Saloon, mounted the outside stairs and knocked on the door of Ingrid's room. He waited impatiently until he heard movement from inside.

'Who is it?' a husky voice called.

'Helmut! Open up for heaven's sake!'

A key rattled, the door opened, and Ingrid appeared, drawing a silk dressing-gown about her, her eyes bleary, brushing back strands of her hair, but her sleepiness vanished when she saw him.

'My God, Helmut, you smell like death and look even worse!'

'Rosa?' he gasped. 'Is she . . . ?'

'*Ja, ja*. She's here. Come in.'

He entered and saw that there was a bed in the room's corner on which Rosa was sitting up. Helmut went to her, slipped his arms around her and whispered '*Meine Kleines Röschen.*' He smoothed her hair, thankful that she was safe. He tried to explain to her what had happened, but it was more for Ingrid's benefit than his daughter's. Rosa just shook her head. It was too much to comprehend.

'Keno's got to do something about this,' Helmut said. 'The railroad can't be allowed to get away with it.'

'Men have been talking in the saloon,' Ingrid said. 'They all believe you set off those explosives.'

'Well, I didn't. And they had no right to wreck my place.' He paused, then he added, 'Have you got some clothes I can put on? I can't go around in a nightshirt for ever.'

She allowed herself the faintest of smiles. She crossed the room to a big cupboard and opened it up. 'Henry won't mind you borrowing something. He's about the same size. He's away on business at present, otherwise he'd have been here.' She hesitated, then went on. 'Helmut, there's something I need to tell you.'

'What?' He went to the cupboard, searched through some fancy suits and shirts until he found some older clothing.

'Henry has asked me to marry him.'

Despite the grimness of all he had suffered, Helmut could not suppress a laugh. 'But you are already married, and bigamy is a serious offence, remember?'

'Only you and I know . . . '

He raised his hand to her lips, stifled her words, aware that Rosa's big eyes were focused on them. It was impossible to know how much she understood. Helmut pulled on a pair of Henry Claypole's pants and a shirt. He also found some old footwear, then he led Ingrid out on to the veranda and closed the door behind them.

'Only you and I know about . . . us,' she continued, and there was a pleading tone in her voice. 'You see, I'm carrying his child.'

In all these years he had never dreamed that such a situation would arise. The boot was truly on the other foot. He slowly buttoned his shirt, deep in thought.

'Then we will have to get divorced,' he said.

'*Nein*! We cannot do that, Helmut.'

'Why not?'

'Henry does not know I was married before. If we divorced, it would all come out. It would probably be in the papers. And anyway, I am Catholic and divorce is not allowed.'

'Nor is bigamy,' he chided. 'You don't think Claypole would marry you, if he knew about us?'

She gave her head a miserable shake.

'Then you are asking me to say nothing,' he said.

'Please, Helmut. It will still be our secret. Nobody else need know.'

'But don't you realize,' he said, 'that it's as much in my interest to keep quiet as it is yours.'

'But we all know what the situation is. Thomas Keno says your woman, Delphinia, is likely to hang.'

'Don't say that!' Helmut retorted angrily. But then he saw how her mind was angling. If Delphinia was hanged,

God forbid, he would have little reason to keep quiet and it would ruin her chances of marriage to Claypole. Right now the prospect of becoming his wife seemed to be the most important factor in her entire life.

He saw his chance. 'Then you must let me have the deeds of the land back.'

She turned away, dropping her eyes. 'I cannot, Helmut. You see, I do not have them. The solicitor who witnessed everything when you had my name put on the deeds . . . well, when he died, I got the deeds to look after myself. I thought they would be safer locked in my drawer than over at that office. And so they would have been. The only trouble was the fire we had here, everything got burned.'

'*Nein!*' he said, hardly able to believe his ears, and then the door opened behind them and Rosa appeared. Helmut's mind was jerked back to his more immediate problems.

'You will look after her?' he asked. 'Just as soon as I've told Keno about the attack on my place, I'll come back and we'll have to decide what's to be done.'

She nodded, put her arm around Rosa's shoulder.

'Ingrid,' he said firmly, 'she must never become one of your girls.'

'Do not worry. I will look after her.'

He left her then, hurrying down the stairs and into Main Street, Claypole's shoes pinching his toes. He realized there was a pocket-watch in Claypole's pants and he determined to return it when he got the opportunity. He found Keno in his long narrow office, his feet on the desk as he read the *Harvest Springs Herald*. Seeing he had a visitor, the marshal came to his feet, his paper dropping to the floor.

'Rapp! Didn't figure you'd have the nerve to show up!'

Helmut said, 'Men from the railroad have burned my place. They've got to be punished.'

Keno gave him a long withering look. 'I guess they had every right to burn your place after what you did to them, killing a man and all.'

Helmut spluttered with indignation. 'I never did that.'

Keno's hand moved swiftly, plucking his gun from its holster and clicking back the hammer in one smooth movement.'

'It's you who will face justice!' he shouted. 'Murderers must run in your family. Husband and wife, eh? Helmut Rapp, I'm arresting you on a charge of killing that railroad man!'

'You're crazy!' Helmut retorted.

'We'll see about that,' Keno cried, jerking his gun menacingly. 'Get yourself in the cell, or I'll shoot you down here and now, damn you!'

Helmut considered twisting around, making a run out into the street, calling the man's bluff — but a glance into Keno's impatient face convinced him that this man was not bluffing. His hand was gripping the gun tightly, his finger already agitating the trigger. Helmut noticed something else. On

Keno's desk, an empty whiskey glass was lying on its side. It had been knocked over when Keno had dropped his newspaper. The smell of whiskey wafted to Helmut's nostrils, but it was not coming from the spilled contents of the glass. It was on Keno's breath. He had always had a reputation for heavy drinking. If he was slightly inebriated, as Helmut sensed, he was likely to do something crazy — like killing a man and counting the cost afterwards, particularly a man already suspected of murder.

'OK, Marshal Keno,' Helmut said quickly. 'You win, this time, *ja*,' and he raised his hands submissively, moved to step past Keno towards the cell beyond. Inwardly his heart was pounding, because he knew he could be dead within seconds. Keno was fumbling for the jail keys with his free hand. Helmut whirled, brushed the gun aside and rammed his fist full force into Keno's jaw, feeling the satisfying crack of bone. The marshal collapsed like a pole-axed bull, splintering his chair, going down with a great clatter on the boarded floor.

Helmut was turning to run from the place, when he remembered Keno's gun. He glanced around, saw that it had fallen beneath the desk. Stooping, he grabbed it and thrust it into his belt. He noticed his knuckles were bloody and painful. Maybe he had broken them at the same time as he had cracked Keno's jaw. He risked a final look at the marshal. His head had caught the side of the desk as he had fallen, was now twisted at a strange angle, blood darkening his face. Helmut wondered if he was dead, but now was not the time to check. He escaped through the doorway and into the street. A blood bay horse was tethered to the hitch rail, its cinch slackened. He hesitated. Somebody called to him from the other side of the street. Glancing across, he saw a man stepping off the boardwalk, breaking into a run. Something on his shirt glinted in the sun — a badge.

He was one of Keno's deputies — Denton.

Helmut did not pause for contemplation. He drew the cinch tight, hooked in the lug and pulled the horse's reins from the hitch rail. Thrusting his toe into the stirrup, he hauled himself into the saddle. At first the blood bay balked, humping its back, but he drummed his heels into its barrel, whipped hard with the reins, and they shot forward, gathering speed as Denton shouted again. *Stop! That's the marshal's horse!* But by now he was away, setting his mount leaping over the wide ditches in the street, dug to stop horse-racing, but they did not stop Helmut and the dust clouded behind him as he raced through the town's outbuildings, scattering chickens and dogs, and on into the prairie beyond.

In addition to accusation of at least one murder, he was now guilty of stealing a horse and a gun. Horse-stealing was considered equal to murder in gravity; both crimes were punishable by the rope, but Helmut gave no thought to the future and its implications. He had bought time. He figured he needed that above all else.

15

Ingrid had waited in her room. She was annoyed that Helmut had failed to return as he had promised. She had hoped that they could have discussed matters at greater length and reached an agreement. The fact was that she no longer cared whether she had Helmut's land or not. She had realized that anything would be very difficult to prove without the copy of the deeds bearing the handover signatures. No doubt the original copy was held by the Land Office in New York, but that had never been altered. Maybe she had been naïve at the time but she had never given it a thought. Anyway, she felt desperate to relinquish her past. Henry was a very wealthy man and she herself had made plenty of money from the saloon and bawdy-house. If giving up her claim to Coldwater Valley cleared the way for her to become Henry's wife, then she was beyond caring. Helmut could keep his land, or at least sell it off.

Now her mind tended to drift to other matters, such as contending with tiresome morning sickness. And one other thing: she was forming an attachment for Rosa. At this moment Rosa was happily sitting at a table looking at pictures in a book and making appreciative babylike sounds. The girl was difficult, but Ingrid had really taken to her, and the feeling was clearly reciprocated for Rosa wore a constant smile. She presented a new sort of challenge to Ingrid, which she somehow welcomed. She had decided that she would keep Rosa if she possibly could. And despite Helmut's wishes, she saw no reason why the girl should not join her own profession. She hadn't the brain for anything else.

She turned as there was a knock on her door and she called, 'Come in!'

Her newest girl, Eva who came from

Hamburg, entered. She was a pretty nineteen-year-old. Her eyes were perfectly round, like a kitten's. She was proving popular with the clients, but right now her usual smile was absent. She obviously had something on her mind.

'Ingrid,' she said and continued to speak in German, 'I feel I should tell you about one of my customers, Greg Higgins — about something he told me.'

Ingrid gave her head a disapproving shake. 'What clients say when they are making love should not be spread around. We'd soon lose all our custom if secrets were revealed. Men are very sensitive in such matters.'

'But this is so important,' Eva persisted. 'It concerns Rosa here.'

Despite the fact that Rosa could not understand German, she heard her name and turned her head.

Ingrid hesitated, then said, 'Well, if it is so important, you'd better tell me, but don't say anything to anybody else.'

The girl took a deep tremulous breath. 'It was last night when Greg Higgins was with me. He told me that he and a man called Joe Briggs were sent out to the Rapp homestead to try and get a paper signed. He boasted how they cornered Rosa and how they both of them raped her, pinning her against a tree. She had acted as if she wanted it, as compliant as a rabbit, but when they gave it to her, she started screaming and her mother came out and shot Joe Briggs dead. Greg Higgins said they were only having a bit of fun and the woman had no rights to start shooting. But she got her deserts, so he claimed. She was taken to Leavenworth to stand trial for murder. I do not think that is fair. She only did what any mother would have done and protected her daughter.'

Ingrid had been listening intently, seeing the implications of the girl's words.

Eva was incensed with the apparent injustice. 'I think that we should tell somebody that Rosa's mother doesn't deserve any punishment. What she did should not be classed as murder.'

Ingrid was shaking her head. 'If you went to the law about this, we would lose half our customers. They treat our girls as confidants.'

'But Rosa's poor mother!' Eva exclaimed.

Ingrid's expression hardened. 'She must stand trial. We cannot afford to lose business because of her.'

She knew there must be some truth in the girl's story. That morning she had taken Rosa for a walk around the town's stores. They had come face to face with Gregg Higgins. Rosa had pointed at him and then run into a store and cowered behind a barrel. Higgins had hurried on while Ingrid rescued Rosa, who was in a highly frightened state until she was given a candy later on.

Ingrid stood up, went to the drawer of her writing desk and took out a Holy Bible. 'Swear on this, Eva, that you will not tell another soul.'

* * *

It was the following afternoon, and Abe Mason was sitting in the marshal's office, studying his Bible. He had just finished reading Proverbs 16.33: *We make our own decisions, but the Lord alone determines what happens . . .*

With Thomas Keno away, chasing the German, Abe Mason was acting marshal of Harvest Springs. He wondered how long Keno would be gone. He had ridden out of town in a blazing fury, all horns and rattles, nursing a jaw the size of a water melon and vowing he was going to track down Helmut Rapp and bring him in, dead or alive, preferably the former. Mason had seldom seen a man so full of hate.

Mason put his Bible down on the desk and glanced at the clock on the wall. A quarter past four. Young Greg Higgins should have relieved him an hour ago but had not appeared. Suddenly aware of his thirst, Mason searched around for the coffee. He couldn't see any. He tried a couple of cupboards, but they were locked. He checked the drawer of the desk and found a key. He had never known such security measures for coffee, but then Keno had always had a reputation for meanness. Mason tried the key in the smaller cupboard. It did not fit. He then tried it in the door of a tall cupboard in the corridor leading towards the empty cells. The key turned, the door swung open, but there was no coffee inside. Something else caught his eye: two sticks of dynamite and some empty packaging. He scratched his head in puzzlement. He couldn't imagine what use Keno would have had for dynamite. The only recent use of such material had been out at the railroaders' camp when somebody had demolished the tunnel and rails — and killed a man.

Mason had lost his desire for coffee. He sat down at the desk again and wondered about the dynamite. He did not trust Keno and had never liked him. He saw him as a greedy and unscrupulous man who was totally unworthy of representing the law. A thought grew in his mind. He tried to push it off, but it would not go away. Supposing Keno had set off the explosion at the railroaders' camp, certain that all suspicion would swing towards Helmut Rapp. Knowing the volatile nature of the workers, it was obvious that they would mount some sort of retaliation against the German, either kill him or send him packing from Coldwater Valley, which was exactly what Keno wanted.

The whole suggestion seemed a bit far-fetched to Mason at first, but gradually he convinced himself of its validity. He felt the one person who would know the truth was young Greg Higgins. He had always been Keno's lackey, doing a lot of his dirty work for him. Higgins was renowned for his vile temper and folks tended to steer clear of him. But he had been appointed as a deputy and right now he was long overdue for his stint on duty.

Mason figured the sooner he quit this wretched job and started on his work for the Lord, the better. He decided he had better go and find Higgins.

Harvest Springs had lapsed into its usual evening quiet — apart from at the Buckthorn Saloon from which the customary jingle of the honky-tonk and assorted revelry emerged. Mason poked his head through the batwings and enquired if anybody had seen Greg Higgins.

A man sitting at a table said, 'I saw him go upstairs about a half-hour ago. Guess he's got a pretty little girl up there.'

Mason nodded his thanks. He had no wish to be seen mounting the inside stairway to the bawdy-house. As, hopefully, a future minister such behaviour would not have been seemly. But one thing was sure. He wanted to remind Higgins it was time he took up his duties.

He went down the side of the saloon into its back yard. It appeared deserted.

The rubbish had been cleared out since the fire had occurred. He knew that some of the girls had their accommodation along the upstairs veranda. For a moment he stood, uncertain, and then suddenly a woman's scream sounded and gurgled to a stop. Mason sprang into action, mounting the stairway two steps at a time. Ahead of him, one of the doors burst open and Greg Higgins rushed out looking as white as death. He was carrying a knife.

Higgins saw Mason, but thrust past him, nearly knocking him over. Mason bridled a curse. Instinct drew him to the open door and he met a sight that made him cry out in anguish. One of 'Heaven's Angels' was sprawled on her bed, the blankets glistening with blood. Her throat was cut so deeply that her head had nearly toppled off. Mason backed away, sickened, knowing the girl was well beyond help. Twisting, he looked over the veranda banister to see Greg Higgins rushing across the yard. Mason snatched his gun from its holster and yelled at Higgins to stop.

Higgins pulled up and swung round, yelling an obscenity. He saw Mason and drew his own gun, firing it immediately. The bullet embedded itself in the roofing close to Mason's head. Higgins was turning to continue his flight, when Mason fired and Higgins threw up his arms, dropped down and lay twitching. By this time the commotion had attracted attention. Doors were opening; girls were emerging in various stages of undress. Somebody discovered the body of Eva and then the screaming started.

Ingrid, rushing from her own room, had rapidly assessed the situation. She stood next to Mason as he holstered his smoking gun. She said, 'I told her to keep her mouth shut about what Higgins told her, but she refused. Apparently she went to Newcombe. Now she's learned her lesson all right.'

Mason gave her an odd look. He was shaken himself. Violence had been the last thing he wanted as he spent his last days as a law-officer. The ease with which he had gunned down a man was daunting. He whispered a quiet prayer to the Lord for forgiveness, but was not certain it would be granted.

Meanwhile a crowd was gathering around Higgins in the yard. Even Sam Newcombe had appeared and was crouching down beside the boy. One glance was enough to tell him he had not long for this world. Blood was frothing on his lips. The bullet must have gone through his lungs.

Mason came down the stairs, shouldered in beside Newcombe.

'Why did you shoot him?' Newcombe asked.

'He'd just murdered one of the girls upstairs. Cut her throat! But why?'

It was Ingrid who supplied the answer. 'Higgins killed her because she betrayed him.'

Newcombe knew this; the girl had visited him that morning at his office. Somebody must have heard as she gabbled out what Higgins had said and word had got back to him, setting his temper aflame.

Mason dropped to his knees beside Higgins. 'Was that true, son?' he asked. 'And was it true that you and Keno set off the explosives at the railroad camp and fixed the blame on Helmut Rapp?'

Higgins gazed up at them, anger colouring his cheeks, despite his poor state. 'Go to hell!' he gasped.

'You might as well come clean,' Mason advised, 'and meet the Lord with a clear conscience.'

A look of fear flashed through Higgins's bloodshot eyes as he felt icy fingers tugging him into the next world. He exhaled a short gurgling sigh, then coughed up some blood. His head dropped back and for a moment it seemed he was dead, but then his lips moved and his words were only just audible.

'OK. It was all . . . all Keno's idea. He hates that German's guts. Wanted to get him off that land any way he could.

187

Now . . . let me die in peace, for God's sake.'

Five minutes later his wish was granted, his eyes glazed over, and the undertaker transferred his corpse to the funeral parlour. Presently, Eva from Hamburg was placed next to him.

16

And so Helmut had fled into wild Kansas, riding Keno's blood bay horse. At first he had been haunted by the belief that he had killed the marshal, that now he really was guilty of a murder. When he realized that Keno was still alive and trailing him, any relief he felt was tempered by the knowledge that the man would be seething with hatred and the lust for revenge. He reminded himself that beyond the sins of his early life, and actions associated with self-preservation, he had committed no crimes worthy of going to his death.

Helmut had been obliged to leave the exhausted horse and struggle on afoot, his weariness almost matching that of the animal. Glancing from elevated ground, he had spotted Keno behind him, getting closer by the minute. Now, finally, with night closing in, Helmut had taken refuge in the narrow draw and had been unable to stave off his tiredness. An indeterminable time later, when Keno's voice boomed out of the darkness, he snapped awake.

'*Helmut Rapp, come out. I know where you are!*'

Helmut gripped the six-shooter. Two shots left, he thought; after that, if I am still alive, it will be bare fists. His heart was pounding; he was afraid that Keno would hear it. He held in his breath, listening, his eyes fixed on the lip of the draw, waiting for the man's head and shoulders to block out the night sky. He had no option but to fight for his life, no option but to greet his hunter with a bullet. And now suddenly he heard footsteps — boots being placed down carefully. Keno must be creeping forward, getting nearer. Helmut crouched, tense as a coiled spring, his gun raised, finger curled around the trigger, straining his eyes for the first sight of a target. He waited.

Eventually he realized that the sound was diminishing. Keno was moving on down the slope, having passed within feet. For a moment Helmut questioned his senses, and then he wondered if Keno was trying some sort of trick to lure him from his hole. Finally, he reached the conclusion that Keno had been bluffing when he had called out, that he had been ignorant of Helmut's exact position, and by remaining still Helmut had called his bluff.

Gradually he relaxed, his heart-pound slowing, feeling cold sweat chilling his clothing. What was Keno playing at? His footsteps had gone quiet. Helmut decided to take a chance. Gingerly, he straightened his aching limbs and raised his head above the lip of the draw, expecting at any second to feel the awful slam of a bullet. None came. Glancing up, he saw how the sky was darkened by cloud. No moon, no stars. Just Keno, somewhere out there in the darkness. If only he could see him, preferably through the sights of the gun.

Knowing that the slightest sound could bring his death, Helmut carefully dragged himself from the draw, hugging the ground as closely as he could. He was sure Keno had gone down the slope — but how far? His own instinct was to try for higher ground. Height was a great confidence booster.

For an age, he lay flat against the ground, feeling the throb of his internal organs, straining his ears for evidence of his enemy's presence. He heard nothing untoward. Glancing upward, he could see the silhouette of the ridge against the lighter black of the sky. He must get up there. It was his only hope. Gripping the gun, he started to snake his way upward. It was then that a pebble squirted out from beneath his foot, clattered down the slope. He cursed and froze, wishing the ground would open up to swallow him. It was obvious that Keno must have heard the sound. Surely, at any moment, the hush would be smashed by the roar of a gun — but he waited, held back on his breath, and there was nothing. He exhaled, started forward again, the revolver tilted up and ready. He moved with the dogged persistence of a snail, his elbows and knees feeling raw as he set his eyes on the ridge above him. He wondered if he was leaving a trail of blood on the rocks. Meanwhile, he was conscious that the sky was showing streaks of paleness. He tried to quicken his progress, but the slope was growing steeper. His body felt as if it were a sack of lead, which he was obliged to drag along. At last he paused for rest.

He was now at the foot of the collar of cliffs that circled the higher ground. Despite his earlier opinion, he realized there were several ways through this wall — narrow gullies caused by the downward gush of spring water from the high peaks. He glanced anxiously around. The sun was getting up, flooding warmth about him and jays were beginning to greet the morning, but otherwise everything seemed quiet with no sign of Keno. Where was the man!

Helmut went forward and lowered himself into the groove of a gully, his feet finding purchase on the cracks within the rocks. The shoes he had borrowed from Henry Claypole were now torn to shreds, not made for the punishment he had given them over the past days. One dropped from his foot, its leather split, its sole little more than one large hole. He shucked off the other and crawled on barefooted. He was glad to be rid of the shoes; they had never been comfortable. It took him ten minutes to climb the steplike ridges within the gully. When he pulled himself out at the top, he lay panting and then listening. All he could hear was the screech of the birds. He inspected his knees and elbows, grunting with satisfaction that the grazes and cuts on them had clotted over.

He glanced ahead, seeing the snow-tipped mountain-peak towering above. He had no idea where he was going or what he would do if he got there. His immediate aim was to escape from Keno, to disappear into obscurity while he pondered on his problems and hopefully came up with some plan, some purpose to all he had suffered. But at this moment his problems seemed too manifold to even consider, apart from eluding Keno.

He was about to climb on when he happened to glance to his left. He gasped with shock. Thomas Keno was crouching in a parallel gully, his red shirt unmistakable. His attention was focused down slope, his rifle resting on the rock before him. He was gazing through some field-glasses. Helmut ducked down, excitement pounding through his veins. He ran his tongue over dry salty lips, fighting to steady himself. Keno was no more than thirty feet distant. Somehow, Helmut must have by-passed him in the darkness. It was obvious that Keno had intended a trick by implying that he had gone down the slope for good, probably making his footsteps loud intentionally. Helmut should have realized that it was all a ruse. But, by nothing less than a miracle, Keno had somehow failed to spot him as he undertook his own crawl.

Fearful that his enemy might twist around, Helmut eased himself a few yards closer, then he threw caution to the wind, stood up, with pistol aimed. He could fire a bullet into Keno's back and put an end to his immediate troubles. But he knew he could not kill a man like this. He was a farmer, not a killer — no more than Delphinia was. Instead, he yelled out. 'Stay where you are, Keno. One false move and I'll shoot you dead!'

Shock jerked Keno's spine rigid. He dropped the field-glasses, but he remained crouched, his head turned away. After a moment he said, 'OK Helmut, you've got the drop on me. I won't try no tricks.'

'Get up!' Helmut snapped, holding the gun with both hands, steadfastly aimed and stepping closer. 'Get up and turn around slowly.'

Keno complied, and Helmut saw that he had two pistols holstered at his hips, butts forward for crossdraw.

'Unbuckle your guns, let them drop down,' Helmut ordered. 'Then raise your hands.'

Keno sighed heavily, slowly fumbled with his buckle and let the heavy weapons drop with a clunk. Helmut watched his eyes; they were darting everywhere, no doubt seeking some way out of his predicament. His face was swollen and heavy with bruising from jaw to temple.

'Guess you sure outwitted me, Helmut,' Keno said. 'That's twice. You'd never do it a third time, though.' He paused, his tongue darting over bruised lips. 'Guess you never realized,' he went on, 'I was coming out to let you know the murder charge against you had been dropped. Unfortunately them railroad workers who wrecked your place have scattered to the winds.

Ain't going to be possible to track any of them down. Still, I guess you'll be glad to hear that with them going absent, the work on the railroad has been slowed right down.'

'They'll start again,' Helmut said, 'just as soon as they can recruit some more men.' He paused, debating the man's words in his mind, then he went on; 'Tell me Keno, if you now admit that it wasn't me who set off those explosives — then who was it?'

'Don't know yet, but as soon as I get back I'll be on their trail for sure.'

Helmut realized that his immediate problems were by no means resolved. If he wasn't going to shoot Keno down, what was he going to do with him? He had no doubt that Keno was lying to him about the murder charge being dropped. He was just biding his time. If he gave him the slightest chance, he would prove as dangerous as a snake.

For a moment they stood gazing at each other, their breathing steadying.

Finally, Keno said, 'My arms sure ache from holding them up. Can't hold 'em up for ever, Helmut. Maybe if we trust each other, we can go back to Harvest Springs and sort things out.' The side of his mouth twisted into a smile.

'Walk back down the slope,' Helmut ordered.

'And my arms?' Keno inquired.

Helmut nodded. 'But I'll have a gun on you. If you try anything, I'll press the trigger.'

'And be guilty of killing a marshal? Then you will have something to stand trial for.' Keno lowered his arms and started down the slope, picking his way warily between the rocks.

Helmut followed, remaining vigilant. He had little doubt that if they did go back to Harvest Springs, Keno would take him into custody, resurrecting the charge of murdering the railroad man.

They scrambled through a gully and proceeded down the slope, both men panting with the exertion of descent. Helmut kept a few paces behind Keno, feeling the heat coming into the day. He felt weary, but there could be no relaxation for him while he had Keno to watch. He suspected that Keno was well aware of this and well content to watch for his chance.

'Where's your horse?' Helmut asked.

Keno pointed down to the prairie below them. 'In that copse of cotton-woods yonder. Where's yours, Helmut — or should I say mine!'

'Left him back aways, so you could find him and take him home. Never wanted to keep something that was not mine.'

'Then you better let me have my gun back,' Keno grunted.

Helmut was not in humorous mood. 'Save your breath for walking.'

They painstakingly covered the mile or so to the trees where Keno had left his horse. Still keeping the gun on him, Helmut unhooked the reata from the saddle and then forced Keno to stand still while he wound it around his arms and shoulders, the marshal objecting that he could be trusted. Helmut ignored him, ensuring that the rope was tightly knotted. He fastened the other end to the saddle horn. He then mounted the horse and ordered Keno to start walking.

And so they proceeded across the rugged country, the sun beating down on them while Keno constantly complained. Several times he stumbled and went down, lying groaning. Helmut was not sure whether he was trying yet another ruse, but he gave him the benefit of the doubt, permitted him time to recover without relaxing his vigilance for a moment. There was a canteen of water hanging from the saddle pommel. He held it to Keno's lips, allowed him to gulp down fluid, then did likewise himself. Several times they stopped for calls of nature. As they started forward again, Keno asked if he could ride the horse for a while, saying his legs were not made for walking.

Helmut said, '*Nein!*' and Keno grumbled that he was a hard man.

'It's the people I know,' Helmut responded. 'They've made me this way.'

'Where you taking me, anyway?' Keno asked.

'We'll stop a while at that tavern. Get some food.'

Keno made no response.

17

True enough, they made it to the tavern in the fork of two trails just as the first flush of evening was softening the sun. Keno was scarlet-faced and exhausted. Helmut, himself utterly weary, realized that he couldn't force the man to go on any longer. As they neared the tumble-down shack, the pot-bellied owner, Bentwell, stepped out on to the stoop, his face showing surprise at the sight of his two visitors.

Helmut knew that both he and Keno needed rest and food, and this seemed the obvious place to seek it.

Bentwell called, 'First customers today,' and then seeing Keno, his jaw sagged with surprise. 'Why you got the marshal tied up?'

'Because he's a dangerous man, that's why,' Helmut responded, sliding from his saddle. 'Now I'd be grateful for something to eat and drink.'

'Sure, mister, no problem. You let your horse drink at the trough. I'll rustle up something.' He stepped back inside his shack.

Helmut wondered if he could trust the man, but eventually decided he had little option. Keno had slumped to the ground, played out. Keeping an eye on him, Helmut led the horse to the trough, and while it sucked at the water, he set about slackening its girth. As he attended to the animal, he had thrust the pistol into his belt. It was the first time he had relaxed his guard, since capturing Keno. The sound of the barman's voice drew his attention. He found himself staring into the muzzle of a long-barrelled rifle.

'You just step across and untie Thomas Keno!'

Helmut cursed, knowing he had been momentarily outfoxed. He heard Keno's croaking laugh, followed by his words. 'Why thanks, Joe. Figured I could rely on you to be a friend.'

'The reward, marshal.' Bentwell kept his eyes on Helmut. 'You said there'd be a big reward. Guess what I'm doing qualifies, eh?'

'Sure,' Keno rasped. 'Sure it does.'

Bentwell spoke to Helmut. 'Before you cut him loose, throw down your gun, mister.'

Helmut sighed deeply. He was standing close to the water trough, and a wild desperation went through him. He could not allow himself to be outwitted now.

'Have it your way,' he grunted. Slowly he moved his hand towards the gun and pulled it from his waistband. 'You sure caught me.'

He saw the start of a smirk on the man's face, and in that instant, he threw himself to the side, blasting off a shot, then another. The barman fired his rifle. As Helmut's bullets splintered the woodwork above the stoop, Bentwell's lead punctured the trough, allowing water to spurt out. Meanwhile, the horse was rearing in panic.

'Kill him!' Keno struggled against the ropes, yelling desperately.

The barman was crouching down on the stoop, fumbling to recharge the rifle. Helmut lifted himself from behind the trough, took aim and guessed he had the other man at his mercy. Bentwell guessed it too. For a fleeting moment they froze, each meeting the other's gaze. The only sound was the gush of water from the trough. Suddenly Bentwell threw his rifle down.

'Don't shoot, mister,' he gasped. 'Never meant you no harm.'

Helmut's gaze swung to Keno. He was still crouched, panting like a dog, his eyes glinting venom. He had used his teeth, somehow worked his hands free of the ropes. His movements clumsy because of the remaining ropes, he straightened himself out and climbed to his feet.

Helmut had briefly turned his attention away from the barman. That was a grave mistake. Bentwell dropped to his knees, clawed up the rifle again and fired. Helmut was hurled back by the hammer-blow of lead into his shoulder. He twisted away, the revolver flying from his grasp. He fell, feeling shock waves radiating through him. He hit the ground hard, his head taking the brunt, sending muzziness flooding through his senses.

Keno saw his chance. He dragged himself to the fallen revolver and grabbed hold of it.

Helmut shook his head, feeling blood pumping out from his shoulder. Wincing with pain, he was trying to force himself up, when he felt the cruel prod of something hard against his head — the revolver barrel. At the same time, Keno's croak of a laugh was in his ears.

'Guess we'll put an end to all this trouble now!' he snarled.

Helmut felt that one way or another he was about to die, but then a sudden hope glowed within him. 'OK, Keno,' he groaned out, 'tell me one last thing. It was you who planted those explosives, wasn't it?'

Keno pressed the muzzle of the gun harder against Helmut's skull, his finger flexing the trigger.

' 'Course it was, you fool. I tricked everybody.'

'But why were you so anxious to get me out of the valley?' Helmut spat the words out through clenched teeth.

Keno's patience was almost stretched to the limit. 'It was Greygoose. He said unless I cleared the way for the railroad, he'd reveal certain things about my past.'

'Kill him, Thomas, for God's sake!' the watching barman cried. Both Helmut and Keno had forgotten him momentarily.

'Goodbye, Mister Rapp!' Keno pulled the trigger.

To have a gun rammed against your skull, even though you are pretty certain there is no bullet left in the chamber, is not a pleasant experience. When the gun emitted a loud click, Helmut knew profound relief. He summoned up his remaining strength to thrust the semi-bound Keno away, then, in no mood for finesse, he dropped on top of him, knees first, feeling ribs cave in. He drove his fist into the already broken jaw, knowing the structure of bone had crumpled under the blow. Keno made no sound. Helmut knew he was not feigning unconsciousness.

The barman had run back into his shack, leaving the gun on the stoop.

Helmut knelt down, rolled the senseless Keno over, and tied his wrists together, pulled them extra tight, then he checked the rest of his bonds. Helmut worked with difficulty, feeling the pain in his shoulder, his hands slippery with his own blood, but he satisfied himself that this time Keno would not wriggle free, even if he was in any condition to do so, which was unlikely.

Leaving him on the ground, Helmut stood up and his heart sank. The rifle had been taken from the spot where it had been dropped. He glanced into the shadowy interior of the tavern, and saw the scrawny woman, Bentwell's wife, holding it in her white fists. She was pointing it not at Helmut but at her husband who was crouching against the bar, glaring malevolently.

'You just stay where you are, Joe Bentwell,' she cried. 'We don't want you sticking your head in no more trouble. I been a widow twice before. I don't want to go through it again.'

'But the reward?' Bentwell gasped hoarsely.

She gave a scornful snort. 'If you believe a word Keno tells you, you're a bigger fool than I took you for!' She swung towards Helmut. 'I think you better be on your way, mister.'

'I need bandage,' Helmut said, 'and some food. And then maybe a little help in getting Keno up on to the horse. He's in no condition for walking.'

The woman nodded, then turned to her husband. 'Get him what he wants, Joe.'

Joe muttered something about 'no-good damned women!', but he got together some victuals, wrapped them in a cloth, and then found some rags for Helmut's shoulder.

Helmut stepped inside the tavern, found a few coins in his pocket and left them on the counter.

The woman came forward. 'Let me do something before you bleed to death!' She pressed the rag over his wound, and tied another strip above it as a form of tourniquet.

Keno was groaning as he returned to him. With great effort, he dragged him to the horse. Under the woman's threat, Joe Bentwell helped Helmut hoist the marshal across the animal's back, like a sack of grain, linking his hands and feet beneath its belly. He would take him back to Harvest Springs. It was a long, hard journey, but now it was one he was determined to make. Perhaps with the town marshal indisposed, he might find genuine justice. Anyway, he needed to make certain that Rosa was all right.

Before they started off, Helmut removed Keno's boots and placed them on his own feet. As he was walking, his need was greater than the marshal's. The boots were a much better fit than Claypole's shoes. He thanked Mrs Bentwell for her kindness, then he led the laden horse forward.

18

It was three tortuous days later when Helmut led the horse up Main Street, Harvest Springs. On the way, he had rested at several small settlements, even got his wound dressed properly. He knew there was lead embedded near his shoulder blade. Keno had recovered sufficiently to sit upright on the horse, though his feet were linked beneath its belly and his hands tied to the pommel of the saddle. He kept groaning, his ribs and the swollen mass of his face were clearly agony, but Helmut felt little compassion and knew that he was still dangerous.

A number of people gathered on the sidewalks to watch as Helmut slowly led his prisoner up the street. He reckoned he was likely to end up in jail himself, that the general belief might still be that he was guilty of the rail worker's death, but right now he was beyond caring. If he was charged with murder, he would fight to prove his innocence. But he was in for a pleasant surprise. Sam Newcombe and Abe Mason stepped into the street to meet him.

'The marshal tried to kill me,' Helmut explained. 'I was obliged to . . . restrain him.'

Sam Newcombe nodded. 'Well, Keno's not the marshal any longer. I fired him as soon as we learned what he had been up to, setting off those explosives and all. Abe, here, is acting marshal in the meantime.'

Mason said, 'I guess we'll put Thomas Keno behind bars, then we'll get the doctor to come over and patch him up, so he's fit to stand trial.'

'Maybe we better get the doctor to look at you too,' Newcombe told Helmut. 'That shoulder of yours is a mess.'

Helmut nodded, thankful at last that he no longer had to guard Keno. He looked at Newcombe and said, 'My girl

Rosa . . . is she all right?'

'Sure. My daughter Susan's been looking after her. We didn't figure it right for her to be at the saloon. Susan's been making a real fuss of her. Rosa's been happy enough, but she's been saying that she wants you and her ma back.'

Helmut nodded, then the implications of Newcombe's words struck him.

'Saying!' he gasped. 'She's started talking again?'

'Sure she has. Told us what happened the night Joe Briggs was killed, about the awful things he and Higgins were doing to her. Reckoned if her mother hadn't come, they'd have killed her.'

Helmut allowed the facts to sink into his brain. Things seemed to have happened so quickly. Certainly, a great burden had been lifted from his shoulders. After a moment he said, 'I'm really grateful to Susan for looking after her,' and then he added, 'Guess you can tell the railroad I accept that offer for purchase of my land.'

Newcombe nodded and smiled. 'You'll be a wealthy man, Helmut. In addition to buying the land, the railroad have talked about compensating you for the destruction of your property and animals.'

Helmut watched as Mason led the sullen Keno away. He felt immensely relieved, but now his thoughts swung to Delphinia. He would know no real peace until she was back at his side.

*　*　*

Over the next few days, the Newcombe family were kindness personified, providing a room for Helmut in their fine house until he could sort his affairs out. He wanted to go to Leavenworth to visit Delphinia. The doctor insisted that he needed surgery to extract the bullet from his shoulder, and, after this was performed, told him that the tissue had been badly ripped but he was lucky it had been a copper bullet. Helmut developed a fever and the doctor told him he must rest, that he could not easily shrug off the exhaustion, shock and infection he had suffered. He would certainly be in no condition to undertake a journey for several days.

Rosa showed real joy at her father's return, kissing him with greater affection than she had shown for a long while. And now she could not stop talking, gabbling away and looking happy.

'Can I have some new chickens, Pa?' she asked.

'Yes, my little rose. Just as soon as we are able.'

Sam Newcombe had told Helmut how, when he had learned the truth about what Higgins and Briggs had done to Rosa on that awful night, he had employed the best attorney he could find, and the latter had assured him that the law would be lenient on a woman who had been protecting her child. She had every right to do that. But it took over a week for the wheels of justice to roll, and meanwhile

Delphinia remained in prison.

Day by day, Helmut regained his strength following the surgery, the fever relenting. He had made up his mind. As soon as he had been paid sufficient money, he would buy land further west. He had no wish to remain in Harvest Springs where Ingrid would be a constant reminder of his past. New land and a new life, hopefully with Delphinia at his side and Rosa maturing into a womanhood where she was protected and loved.

At first, he felt bitter against Ingrid, blaming her for the disasters in his life. If only she had relented her grasp on his land at an earlier time, people's lives might have been saved, Delphinia would not have gone to prison and they could have moved homes without all the havoc that had been created. Why couldn't Henry Claypole have asked her to marry him years ago! But gradually his thinking changed, and he blamed himself for what had occurred. It was he who had proposed marriage to Ingrid in the first place, despite his mother's warnings. He had known full well about her lascivious nature, and he had made the mistake of marrying for lust instead of true love. He had only discovered true love when he had met Delphinia.

As his recuperation continued, he would sit with Abe Mason in the marshal's office, enjoying the man's homely company and discussing the extracts from the Bible that he read out. Like Delphinia, Keno had been taken to Leavenworth to face the legal processes, and William Greygoose of the railroad had seen his chance to glean a reward. He had revealed unwholesome activities in Keno's past, including the murder of a woman in Dodge City.

Helmut's conscience still plagued him. He felt he would never rest until he had confessed his sins to Delphinia, hoping and praying that she would find forgiveness in her heart. So he spent several hours writing out the events of his life in Germany, explaining his weakness, explaining that Ingrid was his first wife, but that she no longer meant anything to him. He pleaded for Delphinia's forgiveness, saying that he loved her above all else. He read through what he had written, tore it up, then rewrote it. But somehow no matter what words he used, he could not alter the heinous fact that he had lured Delphinia into a marriage that was not legal. He was a bigamist, nothing could change that.

My God, he hoped Delphinia would understand — or would the knowledge break her?

Abe Mason asked him what he was so busy writing.

'I've committed a lot of sins in my life,' Helmut explained. 'Things that Delphinia doesn't know about, things that it will hurt her to learn. She might even leave me. But if she doesn't, it would be wrong for us to live with it hanging over us.'

'Why do you want her to know?' Abe

Mason asked. 'Is it because one day everything will come out?'

'No, I don't think so. But I wouldn't want to live with it on my conscience, not any longer.'

'But that would be for your sake, not for hers. Which is worse? Clearing your conscience and breaking her heart, or carrying the burden inside you and preserving her happiness? She's had enough to put up with without adding that to it. Maybe carrying that burden is the punishment for committing them sins in the first place. Maybe some secrets are best kept just between you and the Lord. He'll do the forgiving, not Delphinia. That's what the Holy Bible means in Psalm thirty-two, verse five.'

Helmut thought for a long moment, then his pen scratched on.

'No, Abe. We can't have any secrets from each other when we start our new life. I've got to wipe the slate clean, for better or for worse.'

Abe leaned back in his chair and sighed heavily. He watched Helmut as he finished his letter, carefully blotted it and folded it into an envelope upon which he wrote *Delphinia Rapp*.

Four days later, a telegram arrived for Helmut bearing the joyous news that Delphinia's case was not to be brought to trial, and that she was to be released forthwith. So excited was Helmut, that nothing would stop him from travelling to bring her back. He and Rosa, prettily dressed by Elizabeth Newcombe, were on the stage the following morning bound for Leavenworth.

Helmut was jittery with excitement and Rosa was smiling happily, as they stood in the prison waiting-room. When Delphinia appeared, all three were weeping tears of joy. They hugged each other, and Helmut gabbled out what had happened during Delphinia's absence, and Rosa demonstrated the way her voice had returned. Delphinia was greatly concerned about Helmut's bandaged arm, but he shrugged her concern aside, saying it was healing well, which was true. They were breathless with happiness.

Afterwards, as they drank coffee in a small restaurant nearby, sitting around a table, Helmut took the envelope from his pocket and placed it before her.

'What is it, honey?' she enquired, wondering why Helmut's face had gone suddenly serious.

'Open it,' he said.

Apprehensively, she tore the envelope, extracted the paper from inside. He watched her face as she started to read.

Suddenly she smiled. Kissed the paper as if it was something sweet and laid it down on the table. Sitting next to Helmut, she slipped her arm through his and gazed lovingly into his eyes.

Rosa glanced at the paper, seeing the violet that had been pressed into the corner. Had she been able to read, she would have understood the simple message.

My Dearest Delphinia

Welcome back, my love. I have missed you so much. Now, thank God, we are each other's for ever more.

Your loving husband,

Helmut.

Helmut silently prayed that he had been right in changing his mind and accepting Abe Mason's advice.

THE END